# Fanny Crosby

## Ethel Barrett

**GL**
Regal Books
A Division of GL Publications
Ventura, California, U.S.A.

Published by Regal Books
A Division of GL Publications
Ventura, California 93006
Printed in U.S.A.

**Library of Congress Cataloging in Publication data**

Barrett, Ethel.
    Fanny Crosby

    1. Crosby, Fanny, 1820-1915, in fiction, drama, poetry, etc.   I. Title.
PS3552.A7324I2   1984                   813'.54           83-23064
ISBN 0-8307-0929-0

**3 4 5 6 7 8 9 10 / 91 90 89 88**

Rights for publishing this book in other languages are contracted by Gospel
Literature International (GLINT) foundation. GLINT also provides technical
help for the adaptation, translation, and publishing of Bible study resources
and books in scores of languages worldwide. For further information, contact
GLINT, Post Office Box 488, Rosemead, California, 91770, U.S.A., or the
publisher.

# Author's Note

In writing a biography of a person, it is important to remember that you are writing an *account* of that person's life. You are therefore dealing with facts; there are certain rules to follow and they must never be disobeyed. You cannot add to them, you cannot change them, and you cannot distort them. It is a case of "just the facts, ma'am," and you are stuck with them. The only liberty you are allowed is to leave some of them out if for some reason they distress you or do not seem important.

But in writing a *story* based on a person's life?

Ah, this is quite a different matter. You start out with the facts, to be sure, and you must not change them. But they are only the skeleton. Upon this "skeleton" you must add the muscle and the flesh, to make the story come to life. Sometimes you even take things that happen out of sequence to build up your story, create suspense, make it more interesting. And of course you must invent "dialogue" to make the whole thing a "Story" instead of just a string of facts. And this is a *story*, written in first person.

In writing about Fanny Crosby, I had to "make up" very little. For every incident actually happened just as it is told in this book.

*What?* Organizing a watermelon theft? Deceiving a little blind boy? Impersonating a grandmother? Snatching a great general's sword from its sheath in front of an audience? Saintly little Fanny Crosby?

Yes, indeed.

I simply "juggled it about" a bit.

For instance, I made Fanny's sisters older than they were, when she went home on her vacation. And I introduced Alex earlier in the story than he really appeared in Fanny's life. Actually she met him after she became a (very young) teacher, and not when she was a student. He did propose to her in the garden and she indicated that it was a very romantic moment, but I did make up the dialogue.

Oh, yes, and I did make up the teachers' and students' names.

And in the chapter on little "Teddy," although the anecdote about Theodore Roosevelt is true, the rest of the chapter is "all made up."

Now here is something else, and it is very important. I might have put words in Fanny's mouth, but I did not put attributes in her character that were not there. She did admit to some foibles of human nature in her own writings. She did admit to bitterness over her eye doctor's malpractice, she did admit to anger over Superintendent

Johnson's squelching her. She did admit to her own "cockyness" and pride when she was a student. She did admit to all these things and more about herself. And if her and Alex's love was passionate and strong, their quarrels were equally so. He was more than a match for her, and she relished the fact.

She went through life with all the feelings we have—the joys and frustrations, the good and the bad.

Fanny was no plastic saint.

And it is her total honesty about herself that makes her the more lovable, for she lets us see her humanness.

She came to grips with her blindness by degrees. For years she stoically accepted it; it was not until much later in her life that she was able to actually thank God with all her heart for it.

And what she lacked in sight, she made up for in an acute sense of hearing, an acute sense of touch, and all those "inner vibrations" that only blind people have. And with a far greater awareness than us "ordinary" people. And with—glory be!—a sense of humor!

She "listened" to life with her inner senses. And if it could be said that some of us look at life through "rose-colored glasses"—surely Fanny listened to life through "rose-colored eardrums."

And I suspect that in confessing her few "foibles" she was very, very hard on herself. In any case, I'm sure they all had been pruned away and were long gone by the time, at the age of 91, she saw her Lord "face to face . . . "

# Little Hands

By *Fannie J. Crosby* July 17th, 1875

Little hands were made to labor,
   Little hearts to love and pray,
Little feet to follow Jesus
   In the straight and narrow way.
Hands and heart and feet together
   In their duties must agree,
Cheerful workers, ever toiling,
   Like the busy bee.

Little tongues were made to scatter
   Loving words like music sweet,
Little minds, to keep as treasures
   What they learn at Jesus' feet;
Little tongues and minds together
   In their duty must agree,
Cheerful workers, ever toiling,
   Like the busy bee.

Little eyes were made to sparkle,
   Making all around them bright;
Little souls to live for Jesus,
   Walking in His blessed light;
Little eyes and souls together
   In their duties must agree,
Cheerful workers, ever toiling,
   Like the busy bee.

Jesus tells us we must love Him
   With our heart and soul and mind,
Pleasant work for little children,
   If we ask Him, we shall find.
May our hands be always willing
   And our hearts in love agree,
Cheerful workers, ever toiling,
   Like the busy bee.

# Chapter One

Sometimes adult talk *can* be very boring.

Sitting in our living room, listening to my mother and my Aunt Myra talking, I'm very bored. The only defense against it is to turn them off and go on with my own thoughts as if they weren't there.

So I'm thinking my own thoughts.

There is no doubt about it. Very few girls, or boys, for that matter, have had the fantastic adventures I've had. I've been all over the world, witnessed shipwrecks and wars—I've met kings and princes—

"So this year we've decided to go on an excursion." It's my Aunt Myra's voice. She's sitting over by the window in a rocking chair, talking eagerly to my mother.

I come to with a jolt. This sounds as if it might be good.

My mother's teacup rattles in its saucer as she puts it down on the marble-top table beside her chair. I'm sitting on a hassock by her knee. I say nothing. I've learned that there are times when I can learn a great deal just by listening. They have quite forgotten that I'm here.

"An excursion?" my mother says. "Where?"

"We're not sure, but it won't be the usual picnic. We'll either go for a ride on the lake—or a riverboat ride, perhaps. It's sponsored by the women's guild at the church. Whatever it is, we're going to do something for a change, and not so close to home."

I can't keep my mouth closed any longer. "May I go too?" I cry.

They stop talking as if I'd dropped a bombshell. They suddenly remember that I'm here. I can feel them fumbling for the right things to say.

"Fanny," Aunt Myra says and she's jumping all over her tongue, "we're not sure yet where we're going, but if it is on a boat it will be dangerous."

"That's right, dear," Mother says. "People can't be looking out for you every single minute and you might get into trouble."

"I can look out for myself," I begin, but they both start to talk at once. Mother wins. "Sis," she says to my Aunt Myra, "we have plenty of time to talk about it some other time—not now."

I put my teacup up on the marble table. I'm allowed to have tea if it's half diluted with water. There is a little silence. Then—

"My, it's chilly for May," Aunt Myra says awkwardly. "I'll be glad when warm weather gets here. I wonder where I left my sweater."

"You left it out in the swing, dear," Mother says.

"I'll get it," I say. I get to my feet and head for the door, jumping over another hassock on the other side of the room on the way.

The swing has two-seater seats facing each other with a floor between them. They're all made of wooden slats and hang from a frame. It's a nice place to sit and talk. You make it swing by pushing on the floor. I have to stand up to do this; my feet won't reach the floor when I'm sitting down. I feel on both seats and finally find the sweater on the floor. I grab it and go rushing back in. Too soon. They're talking about me. They didn't expect me back so quickly.

"How does she do it?" Aunt Myra's saying. "She jumped over that hassock for all the world as if she knew it was there."

"Oh, she knew it was there," Mother says. "She knows exactly where everything is. If we can only remember to keep things in the same place."

They stop when they realize I'm at the door.

"Ned is down at the barn," I say, "and the horses are out by the fence. May I go down and feed them?"

"Of course, dear," Mother says. They both seem relieved.

I get a few lumps of sugar out of the sugar bowl and put them in my apron pocket. I run as fast as I can down to the barn—my hair flying behind me.

"Well, Miss Fanny," Ned says when I get there. I don't bother with the gate. I start to scramble over the fence. He swoops me up in his arms and lifts me over the rest of the way and sets me on my feet. "Is this Dobbin?" I say, stretching my hand toward one of the horses.

"Yes, it is," I say, not waiting for him to answer.

"I can tell by his nose." Dobbin stretches his head down toward me. I feel his wet nose. I blow into one of his nostrils. He shivers with delight and blows out like a long sneeze and the air comes out through his lips and makes them wobble. I fish for the sugar in my apron pocket and hold it up to him, remembering to arch my hand and keep my fingers back so they won't get caught in his mouth. He licks at the sugar. His tongue feels like sandpaper. It's a nice feeling.

"May I ride him, Ned?"

"You may *walk* him, Miss Fanny. Don't run him. He doesn't have a saddle on."

He swings me up on Dobbin's back and I grab ahold of Dobbin's mane and clamp my legs across his big back, squeezing with my knees. I can't begin to grip him the way I ought. My legs are too short. I give him a gentle tug on his mane and make a clicking sound. He backs up slowly like a big boat coming out of its slip and I tug at his mane again and give him the signal to run. I know the direction in which he is going. I hear Ned's frantic voice behind us.

"Fan-ne-e-y! You can't see!"

"Oooooh—the horse can!" I call back over my shoulder.

And I'm right. Dobbin knows very well that I cannot see. Riding him is like rocking in a rocking chair. When he gets to the edge of the meadow he slows down and turns gently and heads back toward the barn at a walk.

We talk to each other all the way back to the barn. I talk to him and he snorts back at me. And a couple of times he sneezes. We understand each other perfectly. Dobbin is patient with me and I am patient with him. It's much harder to be patient with people. Sometimes I think people don't understand me at all, even those who love me the best.

*Fanny, you can't do this. You might get hurt. Fanny, you may go to school with your sisters but just for a half day. You can't see anything, you know. You can only listen. Fanny, there's no sense in your going along on the excursion. You won't be missing anything. After all, you couldn't see anything if you did go. So it won't matter whether you go or stay at home, will it, darling?*

I love them all, especially my mother. I would love my papa too, but he died when I was *very* young. I'm five going-on-six now, but I'm a lot smarter than they think I am. Or is it that they *do* know how smart I am and it scares them a little? Maybe God made me extra smart to make up for my blindness. Of course, all the adventures I've had, and the people I've met—they aren't for real. They are the people I've met through all the things that have been read to me, especially the Bible, but they're real to me. They're the world I live in—a whole other world apart from the people around me I can touch and hear. But my family and friends don't understand me at all. All they can think of is that I'm blind. My world is all dark gray. And people and things are just shapeless blobs of darker gray.

I think about all this after Ned lifts me down and scolds me gently and turns me in the direction of the house so I can go back. I think about it all the way back to the house. It's ridiculous. I'm going to have a talk with God about this. There are a lot of things we need to straighten out. Here I am, surrounded by people who love me, and the only one in all the world who really understands me is a horse.

# A Child of Jesus

By *Fanny J. Crosby*, 1872

A child of Jesus! O how sweet
   These precious words to hear;
No music breathed by mortal tongue
   Was ever half so dear.
A child of Jesus! blissful hope
   That fills me day by day
With joy the world can never give,
   And never take away.

A child of Jesus! near the cross
   My soul would still abide,
And feel, beneath His watchful care,
   Its every want supplied.
A child of Jesus, happy thought!
   Be this forever mine,
To see, through every gathering cloud,
   My Father's glory shine.

A child of Jesus, owned, and blessed
   By Him who died for me;
His wondrous love, His pard'ning
   grace,
   My song in heaven shall be;
A child of Jesus! O how sweet
   These precious words to hear;
No music breathed by mortal tongue
   Was ever half so dear.

# Chapter Two

I haven't gotten around to my talk with God yet, and it's been a couple of weeks. I don't mean I haven't been praying; I pray every night with Mama. We do it aloud which is a good idea because then we know what each other is thinking. And it doubles the strength of our prayers. It's sort of ganging up on God.

But my real talks with God are different. They are very private and some of them are very, very secret.

But anyhow, the reason why I keep postponing this talk is that I have a lot of complaints to make and when I'm going to complain I like to get my thoughts all marshalled so I won't say anything I'll be sorry for. It's very dangerous to complain to God just out of the top of your head. You can get yourself in a lot of trouble that way. He just might take you up on some of the things you're griping about and decide that if this is the way you want it, this is the way you're going to get it. And it may not be what you wanted after all. So I was postponing that talk 'til I knew what I wanted to say.

Then something happened that knocked the whole idea of the talk right out of my head. It happened about a week after I rode Dobbin and got told that I couldn't go on the excursion.

I took off by myself and climbed my favorite tree for sulking. I can climb a tree as well as anybody, once I get acquainted with it. And Mama lets me climb along with the rest of the children as long as they are with me. But this is my own private tree. And it's a great tree to sneak off and be quiet in whether I'm sulking or not.

I also conduct huge choirs there. I can coax the most beautiful music out of the birds and the wind and the rustling leaves. The wind can laugh or cry or moan or sing beautiful melodies while the leaves rustle a counterpoint—more beautiful than anything anyone has ever heard before—more beautiful than some of the tunes they sing in church or in Aunt Myra's Victrola.

Anyhow, I was conducting this huge choir. There was no wind and no bass notes, just treble. We were just beginning to get into the spirit of the thing when I heard Mama's voice calling. "Fanny," she called. "Where are you?"

I called back real loud, even before I started to shimmy down the tree. I always do that because everybody worries about me. So if I don't answer right away, they're sure they're going to find me facedown in the creek or something horrible like that. She was calling from the front porch. I got there as fast as I could.

"I have something for you, Fanny," she said. "You'll have to sit down on the porch steps before I can give it to you."

I sat down.

"Hold out your arms," she said. I held out my arms, waiting.

"Is it a toy?" I asked.

"It's not just any toy," she said. "It's a *live toy*." And she put it in my arms. It was soft and warm and I could feel it trembling under my touch. Whatever it was, it was frightened. I felt its head, its ears, its wet little nose. "Is it a puppy?" I asked.

She did not keep me guessing. "It's a lamb," she said. She explained that it was all mine, completely mine and it would not belong to anyone else ever.

I scarcely heard her. I felt it from tip to toe—its soft little face, its rough little tongue, its ears, its wet nose, its baby hoofs, its funny little tail, wagging like mad.

And that's why I hadn't gotten around to having that talk with God except to thank Him, of course. I'm sitting here in the grass halfway between the house and the barn and Wooley (yes, I named him Wooley) is wobbling about in the grass beside me. I'm thinking seriously of asking if I can take him to school so I can be like the little girl in the poem. I've even thought of asking Mom if I can have my name changed to Mary. But Wooley is too much of a baby to take that far, and anyhow, school will be out in a couple of weeks and my sisters and my friends will be around all day. I'll let them help me take care of Wooley and maybe even let them play with him a little bit, but no one else can *own* him. He's absolutely all mine and nobody else's. I don't think I have ever been this happy in all my whole life.

# Stand Up for the Right

By *Fannie Crosby* Apr. 15/98

The eyes of the world are upon us;
  O Christians, awake and beware!
Look well to our lives every moment,
  Be faithful, and watch unto prayer.

*Chorus:* Avoid the appearance of evil;
    The path of the righteous pur-
    sue.
    Stand up for the right and
    defend it;
    To Jesus be loyal and true.

The eyes of the world upon us;
  Keep close to the side of our Lord.
Remember the perfect example
  He left in His excellent word.
                 *Chorus.*

The eyes of the world are upon us;
  But He, our Redeemer and Friend,
Has promised His own to deliver,
  And carry them safe to the end.
                 *Chorus.*

# Chapter Three

It was the most glorious summer of my whole life. But now it's over—everything is over.

I'm sitting on the two-seater swing out on the porch, my hands folded in my lap. I don't feel like pretending I'm a boat captain announcing the ports as the boat goes rushing through the waters. Or that I'm a wagon train captain, braving the elements as I lead my people to safety.

The rest of the family are inside eating supper. Mama comes out stepping softly, and tucks a sweater around me. "I'm sorry, darling," she says. I don't answer. She goes back in the house without another word.

The air is nippy. I think of the summer, now gone—a summer when I was Wooley's and Wooley was mine. I played with him morning, noon and night. I tried to teach him tricks but that didn't work out too well. Lambs just aren't that smart. But Wooley was just about as smart as a lamb could possibly be. His idea of fun was to get a good start and then run pell-mell into me and butt me with all his might. It was the game we played more often than any other. Sometimes the kids would even watch and help us play it. "Here he comes, Fanny," they'd yell.

The days rolled into weeks and weeks, but we never got tired of playing the game. We were so busy having fun that none of us realized that Wooley was getting bigger and bigger with every passing week. At first, when he began butting me so hard I couldn't stay on my feet, we all laughed louder than ever. And then the day came when he butted me and I fell down so hard that it jarred my teeth. I laughed about it but my laugh was shaky. I wouldn't admit it to anyone but he had really hurt me.

After a while the kids got tired of the game, and I was just as glad, for this butting business was getting less and less funny. Nobody enjoyed it anymore. Nobody, that is, but Wooley. Everybody started keeping an eye on him then and to stop him when he backed off, dug his front hoofs into the ground and prepared to attack. But they couldn't keep their eyes on him every minute. So I was down more than I was up.

I always forgave him though, but our reconciliations were sometimes painful. Once I forgave him with a tooth through my lower lip.

Mother watched all this. And worried.

"Fanny, we can't keep on like this," she'd say. "We must do something about Wooley."

"But he's my lamb, Mama," I'd say. "And I've

loved him all through his lambhood."

"Fanny, let's face it," she'd say. "It's no longer his lambhood. It's his sheephood. He's not a gentle little lamb anymore. He's a belligerent old mutton-head and you know it."

"But, Mama, he's my friend," I'd wail. "He's given me something to live for. For the first time in my life I feel as if I'm going places—"

"You're going places all right," she'd say. "All over the yard, clear down to the barn, and you're going to wind up in the hospital if we don't do something about Wooley."

It wasn't too long after that when Wooley disappeared. Just plain disappeared. No one seemed to know where he had gone. No one. Not Mama or Aunt Myra or Ned or any of the grown-ups. Not even Grandpa when he came to visit.

It wasn't until tonight that I found out where he was. I came in late for supper. I had been hunting for him down in the south pasture. I'd been there a hundred times before but I never gave up looking. He knew my voice and I knew his. And I was absolutely certain that I would still find him, his foot caught between rocks or something. And I would rescue him and lead him triumphantly home and there would be great rejoicing forevermore.

Mama didn't ask me where I'd been or scold me for being late. She just started filling my plate while I washed my hands and sat down in my place at the table. "What's for supper?" I asked innocently. There was a silence so thick I could have cut it with a knife.

"Lamb chops," my sisters said together. I heard the clatters and jingles as everyone got suddenly busy and someone put my plate in front of me. I already knew the horrible truth, but I had to be sure. I scanned the food on my plate with the tips of my fingers. I felt the familiar shape of a lamb chop.

"WOOLEY!"

Grandpa was there and he tried to help. "Now, Fanny—" he began softly, but I wouldn't let him finish.

"That's Wooley," I wailed. "I'd know him anywhere. He was condemned without a trial."

"Fanny dear—"

"He was condemned to death with no one to plead his case."

"But—"

"That's *cannibalism*. Wooley was practically human."

"Now, honey—"

I didn't wait to hear any more. I dashed out of the house and no one tried to stop me. Now I'm sitting in the swing, shivering. For even with a sweater on the air is nippy. In a few days all the kids will be going back to school and I'll be totally alone again. I begin to talk to God and I don't even care if anybody comes out of the house and hears me. I can't wait until I go to bed. We have to have this out right here and now.

*God, that's a terrible thing these people did to me. They gave me Wooley and they thought when he was little that everything he did was cute. When he got big and did the very same things everybody got mad at him. He was only doing what he had been doing all his life. But if they were going to kill him, the least they could do was to let me know. I suppose they didn't dare. Mama knew I'd raise the roof. God, I'm sadder than I've ever been before. Do people ever die of sadness? I think I'm going to die of sadness.*

*But while we're at it, God, I'm angry too, and I don't want to die of anger. But the kids are going back to school and learning things and the whole world is rushing by and I'm not going anyplace. I'm just left here in darkness.*

"Fanny." Mama's calling. I don't answer. I know she can see me over here in the swing. She just wants to find out if we're still speaking. She comes over to the swing. It jiggles as she steps into it. She sits on the seat facing me for a minute. Then she comes over and sits by me. She starts to take me in her arms. I tighten up. I want to pull away. I don't want anyone to love me.

"I hate that doctor who ruined my eyes and made me blind," I bellow. She doesn't answer. She understands. I don't hate the doctor or anyone else, for that matter. She knows I really don't hate anybody. I just have to let off some steam.

We rock back and forth in the swing without talking, our arms around each other. My nose is running now. I fish in my apron pocket for a handkerchief. She waits till I blow my nose. Then, "Fanny, I have a surprise for you," she says. "I wasn't going to tell you about it until I was sure of the appointment. I was afraid you would get too excited. We're going to see some doctors about your eyes."

All my insides tighten up. It was a doctor who ruined my eyes and made me blind when I was an infant. I don't want to see any more doctors about my eyes. I tell her so.

"But this is different, Fanny," she says. "These

doctors are specialists and they are surgeons."

"Surgeons? Surgeons cut people. What would they do to my eyes, Mama?" I ask.

"It would be a delicate operation," she says, "but we're not sure they're going to do anything at all. They've got to examine your eyes first and then we'll see."

"But—but—who, but where and who are they? There are no surgeons around here."

"That's the exciting part of it, Fanny," my mother says. "You've always wanted to travel. Well, you're going to. They're in New York City."

"New York City, Mama? Way down there? Miles and miles and miles? The big city, you mean?"

"The very same," she laughs. "It's the most exciting city in all America."

I draw my knees up and hug them while we swing back and forth as we talk about it. Mama tells me how she heard about the doctors and how she came to write for the appointment. She expects to get an answer back any day now. We talk until Grandpa comes out on the porch. It's past my bedtime.

"I'll take you up, Fanny," Grandpa says, "and hear your prayers, if you want me to. I've got your candle lighted."

I start to say something and then stop. It's no use explaining to them that night is the same as day to me and that I don't need to be "lighted" upstairs to my room. I can see better than any of them in the dark.

Gramps sits in the rocker up in my room by the window while I get myself ready for bed. I sink in up to my chin in my feather bed. I usually plump my pillows up and sit up for a little talk, but tonight I don't feel like it. I lie down flat. Gramp comes over and stands by my bed.

"Want to talk about it?"

"About what?"

"Oh, anything. Want me to hear you say your prayers?"

"No, Gramp, I already talked to God down in the swing. I'd rather talk to Him alone tonight up here."

There's a long silence. I know Grandpa feels terrible. I can feel it. I draw my knees up and hug them and wait.

"You know they had to do it, Fanny," he says at last. "Wooley was really getting dangerous. He was big, bigger than you realize and getting fierce. They did it for your own safety."

"They should have told me."

"They probably hoped you'd never find out and just think he got lost."

"I don't want to talk about it, Gramp."

He stands there for a minute in silence. Then he leans over and kisses me. His whiskers are soft and clean smelling. His face is soft too, like old wrinkled leather. I love his face. I think he must be a strong, beautiful man. "My little Fran, my best girl," he says. And then in a minute he's gone. I turn over on my side and say good night to God.

*God, thank you. I thank you that you are going to let me go to the big city of New York. I'd like to be happy about it, but I can't be happy about anything right now with Wooley dead. He's gone and I know I can't bring him back, but I'll never, never, never, never eat him, not even if I starve.*

I lie there thinking for a long time. I try to think

of something to be glad about concerning Wooley. It's hard for he's dead, and my heart is broken. *But at least,* I think after a while, *I don't have to worry that he is out there caught in a trap maybe, crying out for me to come and find him.* That would be the worst thing.

As for the trip to New York City—forget it, for now. I don't intend to be happy about anything right away. For a friend like Wooley I should go into mourning for at least a week.

# The Way Before Me

By *Fanny Crosby*, Nov. 16-94

I know not the way before me,
　　But Jesus will guide me still;
And so, in His mercy trusting,
　　I patiently wait His will.

*Chorus:* I know not the cares or sor-
　　　　　　rows
　　　　　　That into my life may fall,
　　　　　　But Jesus, my loving Savior,
　　　　　　Will give me the grace for all.

I know not the way before me,
　　But Jesus my Lord is near,
To shelter, protect and keep me;
　　Then why should I doubt or fear?
　　　　　　　　　　　　*Chorus.*

I know not the way before me,
　　But this to my soul is given—
The promise of life eternal,
　　A home and a rest in heaven.
　　　　　　　　　　　　*Chorus.*

# Chapter Four

It's a soft dawn of a summer morning and I'm about to begin my great adventure—the greatest adventure of my life so far. Mama and I are sitting in the waiting room of a little town on the banks of the Hudson River. We rode here from home in a market wagon. There was no other way we could get here. There are no stages from where we live to any part of the Hudson River.

Grandma and Grandpa are back home staying with my sisters. They've gone back to school. Mama and I are on our own. It's both scary and exciting, for we are waiting for a boat—*a boat*—to take us down to New York City.

The name of this town is Sing Sing. I don't know what gave me the idea that everybody who lives here belongs to a giant choir. But this is the way I pictured it. Mama just told me that this town is no more musical than any other. And I'm disappointed. I guess nobody sings here but the birds. I wonder why they named it Sing Sing. Mama doesn't know either.

In a minute it doesn't matter, for there's a man calling out the announcement that the boat is ready. Mama stands up and her petticoat rustles as she smooths out her skirts and talks to somebody about our baggage. And we start walking. I cling to her hand for I'm not on familiar ground here. And I can't be as cocky and sure of myself as I am when I'm home on my own turf. We walk up to get on the boat but it's not stairs. It's like walking up a hillside. Mama says it's a gangplank.

I know the minute we are actually on the boat. Everything under my feet feels different. It's sort of a swaying motion like being rocked in a cradle or standing up in our two-seater porch swing. *Nothing is firm.* Everything keeps moving. I hang on tighter to Mama's hand.

It's a while before we get settled in the room where we have two bunks and some drawers that are built right into the wall. It is so tiny we can hardly turn around. Mama says it's dark in here, but I wouldn't know the difference. I am so excited my breathing is all crooked.

There is all sorts of shouting outside and the boat begins to move. Mama says the boat is called a *sloop* and that they have just unfurled the sails and we are on our way. I'm so excited I think I might even throw up. I'm beginning to feel strange in my stomach.

Mama sinks down on her bunk and lets go of my hand. I reach out for my bunk too, hanging on to the edge. This is the scariest sensation I've ever had in all my life.

Mama and I had lunch in our little room—at least I had lunch. Mama is seasick. I've had plenty of chances to get acquainted with this sloop. Mama is too sick to watch me very closely. A sloop isn't a real big boat, but it's pretty big for a riverboat. Captain Green has dubbed me first mate of the sloop. I've been getting acquainted with him and with the other passengers on the sloop. Captain Green asked me to sing for him—I like to sing. At first my voice was squeaky because I was a little bit scared. But now I'm belting out songs—every song I know.

> I wish I was a Yankee's wife,
> And then I would have somethin',
> Every fall an ear of corn
> And now and then a pumpkin!

I sang a lot of other songs too. Pretty soon I started charging the passengers a penny each for the songs. Mama is still down on her bunk, seasick—only, in a sloop on the Hudson River, I guess you'd call it riversick. So she isn't around to make me behave. And Captain Green doesn't seem to mind that I'm getting paid for singing. I'm thinking of raising my price. I feel so good I think I could fly. I can't stop singing and I can't stop talking. Everyone keeps telling me how pretty I am and how smart. I'm sorry when it's bedtime and it all has to stop.

Snuggled up in my rocking bed I try talking to Mama. I just can't stop talking, even though Mama doesn't feel like talking to me.

I'm pretty. Everybody loves me. I have a beautiful voice. And I'm smart. And when Dr. Mott and Dr. Delafield get through with me I'll be able to see for myself how great I am. I don't see how I can ever get to sleep.

New York City! The sounds! Oh, the sounds! Sounds I've never heard before. I keep standing up in the carriage as the horses' hoofs clippity clop down the cobblestone streets of this great city. I'm so excited I can hardly stand it. When our sloop docked, Captain Green and all my new friends said good-bye with cheers and laughter and told me they were absolutely sure that very soon I would be able to see.

We stayed last night at Jacob Smith's house on number 10 Roosevelt Street. The Smiths are old family friends. Their house is bigger than ours and Mama says it's fancy and I've never been in such a lovely house before.

But now we're on our way, riding in their fancy carriage. "Sit down, Fanny, before you fall down," Mama keeps saying. The horses' hoofs don't sound at all the way they sound on country roads. The sharp, clicking rhythm is beautiful—just like a poem. A policeman blows his whistle as we pass the corner and something—Mama says it's a trash can is rolling down the street.

When we finally pull up to a stop, the carriage driver helps me out. I grab Mama's hand again and hold on tight while we go up the steps to the front door of Dr. Mott's office. Mama says it's in a block where all houses are attached together. And they all have the same kind of steps and the same kind of fronts. She says they are called brownstone houses or blockhouses.

"I smell geraniums," I tell Mama.

"You're right, Fanny. They're in flower boxes under the windows."

We take one more step forward.

"There is a huge knocker on this front door," Mama says. "I'm going to knock with it right now. Don't let the noise scare you."

I can tell by her voice that she's the one who's scared.

I'm not scared at all. I might be scared of the pain when they operate on my eyes, but it will be worth it, for in a little while I shall be able to see! In a minute someone will open the door and I shall walk into a brand new world.

# Lord, Here Am I

By *Fannie Crosby* Aug. 15th, 1877

Master, Thou callest,
   I gladly obey;
Only direct me,
   And I will away.
Teach me the mission
   Appointed for me,
What is my labor,
   And where it shall be.

*Chorus:* Master, Thou callest
        And this I reply,
        "Ready and willing,
        Lord, here am I."

Willing, my Savior,
   To take up Thy cross;
Willing to suffer
   Reproaches and loss.
Willing to follow,
   If Thou wilt but lead;
Only support me
   With grace in my need.
          *Chorus.*

Ready for labor,
   While life shall remain;
Ready for trials,
   Affliction or pain;
Ready to witness,
   My Savior, for Thee;
Ready to publish
   Thy mercy to me.
          *Chorus.*

Living or dying,
   I still would be Thine;
Yet I am mortal
   While Thou art divine.
Pardon, whenever
   I turn from the right;
Pity, and bring me
   Again to the light.
          *Chorus.*

# Chapter Five

Inside the doctors' office Mama takes a couple of steps and then falters and stops. She leans over and whispers to me. "It's dark in here," she says. "My eyes haven't gotten used to it yet." The nurse's starched apron swishes as she leads us both through some double doors—the kind that slide together—into a waiting room. There are several other patients in the waiting room, but they're all grown-ups, Mama tells me. I am the only child. It smells strange in here, like medicine. But there's something else in the air.

"Why is everybody so afraid of Dr. Mott?" I whispered to Mama. She shooshes me and leans over close to my ear. She whispers that he is such a great doctor that everyone is in awe of him. They hang on his every word. They treat him as if he were some sort of a god. I listen for a while to the other patients talking. They speak in whispers as if they were on sacred ground. They talk as if they know each other and have been there many times before. They discuss Dr. Mott's and Dr. Delafield's marvelous feats of surgery. They use big words I can't understand. But I know I shall never forget them even if I don't know their meaning. I remember just about everything I ever hear, whether I understand what it means or not.

When it comes our turn to go in, a nurse and Mama both take my hands. I can't understand why they're both afraid of the two great doctors. The nurse introduces us.

I'm upset with Mama because her voice trembles as she says hello. But to me people are people and they either please me or they don't. I don't know whether they're great or not. Actually, the greatest man I know is my own grandpa. So I look up and smile to show that I like them and to show them how brave I am.

Dr. Mott takes me up on his lap. He tells me his name again and lets me feel his face. He has a short-cropped beard and a fine big nose. His eyes are deep-set and he has all his hair. I touch his hair lightly so I won't muss it. I can tell, both by his voice and by his face, that he is a kind, gentle man. Dr. Delafield comes close and holds his hand out for me to feel.

Then the doctors lift me up on the table. They start examining my eyes. They both talk softly to me all the while. Now, Fanny, this. And, now, Fanny, that. And, now, Fanny, we're going to do so-and-so. Don't be afraid.

And now I hold my breath waiting to hear what they will say as they begin to talk to Mama. They ask her questions and she answers with words like "poultices" and "drops" and they make little sounds down in their throats as she tells them how the doctor had treated my eyes for an infection when I was six weeks old. There is a little silence. We wait.

Then, "There is nothing we can do for this child's eyes," Dr. Mott says to my mother. "Malpractice has spoiled them—spoiled them for good."

He goes on explaining why this is so. But I don't hear. My mind has ground to a halt. After they finish talking they lift me from the table and set me back down on my feet. They pat my head and say things like, Poor little girl, and God bless you, and We're sorry.

Mama is crying softly. Both of the doctors and the nurse say nice things to her. She blows her nose. I do nothing. Maybe they think that I don't fully understand what they said. But I do understand.

It's just that there's one thought in my head and it's so big there isn't room for anything else.

It's hopeless.

I am blind for life.

I go through all the motions of shaking hands and saying my good-byes and thank yous. But the real me is down inside waiting until I can be alone with it. It is too terrible to share with anyone else.

I am lying on my bunk in the sloop. Except for different passengers, everything is just about the same. Captain Green is as kind and jolly as ever, so I don't let him know how I feel. Mama is so brokenhearted. I wouldn't dream of letting *her* know how I feel. I still think she thinks I don't fully understand yet and she's waiting until we get home to explain it to me better. But I do understand. I got it, every word of it. I know what *malpractice* means. And I know what *hopeless* means. Malpractice means the doctor did the wrong thing to my eyes and ruined them. And hopeless means forever.

I say good night to Mama and we stretch our arms out between our bunks and clasp hands and say our prayers. There are two of me now—the outside me and the inside me. The outside me says prayers with Mama and then we let go of each other's hands and roll over and go to sleep.

*God, it's the inside me talking. I haven't been alone with you for a long time. In one way it seems like a long time—in another way it seems like only a few seconds. You already know it but I have to say it. I am blind for life. I am blind for life. No matter how many times I say it, it doesn't make sense.*

*God, the whole world is rushing by me. Everyone else is doing something important. Everyone else is going somewhere. My sisters and the other kids are going to school and they're learning to be doctors and carpenters and nurses and housewives and teachers.*

*God, I want to forgive that doctor. Then I want to put him out of my mind and never think about him again. I've asked you to give me my sight. I've asked you again and again. And I thought sure when we made this trip that you were going to do it.*

I lie still for a while, thinking about what else I can say to God. I listen to the gentle slurp, slurp of the waves hitting the sloop. I pick up my thoughts.

*. . . that you were going to do it,* I say again. *I mind this. I mind it very much. There's no way I can be happy about it. But there's something else I mind a lot more.*

*God, I haven't got a job to do. If you give me a job to do—I don't care what it is—I promise you that I will do it with all my heart.*

I am quiet for a minute. Now the slurp, slurp is much louder than before. The waves seem to be singing to me. They seem to be telling me not to be discouraged. I sit up in my bunk to listen. They are singing! "Fanny, be brave! Fanny, be brave!"

I can scarcely believe this. My "inside" eyes open wide with amazement. I strain forward listening. The song goes on, "I have a job for you, Fanny. Brighter days are yet to come."

I sit up for a long time in wonder. I don't think I'll tell anybody about this, not for a while. Nobody would believe me.

We've been home for a week now. For once I haven't talked much. But I'm not sulking, it's different.

Mama and Grandpa and Grandma—and even my sisters—know that something wonderful has happened to me. They don't ask any questions. They are all just relieved that I'm not sad.

Yesterday Mr. Drew stopped by our house. He's a drover—and he often goes by our house with herds of sheep and cattle. Anyhow, yesterday he stopped by our house and came up to the front porch. I was sitting in the swing with Mama and Grandma, helping them shell peas. They both "o-o-o-hed" as he came close to the swing.

"Hold out your arms, Fanny," Mr. Drew said. I did. And he placed something on my lap. It wiggled and squirmed and licked my hands. It was a very familiar feeling.

It was a baby lamb.

Grandma and Mama oh'd and ah'd and cooed with delight while I ran my hands gently over the little lamb's warm body. Then I lifted him back up to Mr. Drew. I told him he was very kind and I thanked him with all my heart.

"But I can't take him, Mr. Drew," I said. I tried to explain why. The only words that could come out were, "There can never be another Wooley."

I must have said it just right because I could feel that no one was angry with me. Surprised, yes. Angry, no. Everybody said more things after that—you know—polite things back and forth. And then Mr. Drew said good-bye and took the lamb back down to the road with him.

We went on shelling the peas in silence for a minute and then, "Some things can't happen more than once," I explained to Mama and Grandma. "This was my golden summer, and besides, I don't need a lamb anymore."

Well, that was a mouthful. And I suppose it will take them a while to try to sort out what I mean. But I know what I mean. And besides I know there are two of me now—an outside me and an inside me. And the inside me is in tune with God like it has never been before. And instead of feeling sorry for myself, I feel *special*, for the river waves have sung to me.

And I know that they are God's.

And that I have heard His voice.

By *Fannie Crosby* March 27th, 1876

How bright with song, how full of joy
    Our merry festive day,
And while the moments one by one
    In beauty glide away—

*Chorus:* Once more a happy chorus
        join,
        Ring out, each heart and
        voice!
        Exalt our one triumphant
        Lord,
        And in His name rejoice.

Today the springs of true delight
    Are flowing pure and clear;
Today will be a sunny spot
    Through many a coming year.
                    *Chorus.*

And now, beneath the glowing sky
    Of this our native land,
Let each resolve, for Christ the Lord,
    Like heroes brave to stand.
                    *Chorus.*

"All hail the banner of the cross,"
    Our parting song shall be;
"All hail the banner of the cross,
    For Christ has made us free.
                    *Chorus.*

# Chapter Six

"Mama, the rain has stopped. Is there a rainbow?" I call down to Mama from my upstairs bedroom in Bridgeport, Conecticut.

"Fanny! You should be getting dressed!"

"Is there a rainbow?" I ask again.

"Yes," she calls back, "and it's a beauty. Are you getting dressed, dear?"

"I'm already dressed, Mama. I just want to stand here awhile and think. How much time?"

"We won't be leaving for an hour."

"Oh, great. I'm all ready. I'll be down after a while."

We moved here to Bridgeport to live with the Hawleys when I was nine. I'm fifteen now. I've loved every single minute of it because I was learning so much and discovering so many new things. But I've missed Grandpa and Grandma. That's been the only bad part about it.

I sit in my rocker by the window and look out. I can smell the wet grass after the rain. I can imagine all the birds fluffing out their feathers to dry them out. And I can see that rainbow with my inside eyes. The colors are absolutely beautiful. It's the rainbow that makes me think of Grandma.

It was Grandma who took me up on the brow of a little hill after a rain and "showed" me the rainbow and explained it to me—how it was God's promise to Noah after the flood.

She explained about all the colors in the spectrum. Sometimes when the light is real bright, I can *sorta* see colors. But so faintly that I don't know if I really can or if I'm imagining it. Anyhow, the colors I see with my inside eyes are the ones I go by. In my mind I connect each color with music. The pale light colors are high tinkling notes and the deep rich colors are the bass notes. I even see the shades in between the colors as sharps and flats.

Anyhow, Grandma and I had many sessions in those days about colors, and I wouldn't say anything because I wouldn't want to hurt her feelings, but I was absolutely sure that my colors were more beautiful than hers.

Grandma taught me all about birds too. She described every single kind—their colors and their singing notes.

Grandma and Mama have always read to me from everything they could get their hands on, and from the Bible especially. But after that doleful pronouncement that I would be blind for life, they dug into it with a vengeance. Now I know more of the Bible by heart than all the rest of the family—

and all my friends too—put together.

And I also began to pay closer attention to the singing in church. I can pick out and memorize every verse, every word—no matter how poorly they're sung, which they nearly always were in our church. The people could slither over those words as if they were reading the *Farmers' Almanac*. The words didn't seem to mean any more than that. But I could pick out every one and they meant a lot to me. More and more as time went by.

I could pick out every word the preacher said too, and that was a miracle in itself, for he could say "Jerusalem" in one syllable.

Oh, and I began to write poems about then, too. My very first poem went like this:

Oh, what a happy child I am,
Although I cannot see!
I am resolved that in this world
Contented I will be.

How many blessings I enjoy
That other people don't!
So weep or sigh because I'm blind,
I cannot, nor I won't!

That was surely no literary feat, but it meant a lot to me, so I wrote it after I heard God's voice in the waves.

After we moved here to Bridgeport, Mrs. Hawley took up where Grandma had left off. She did not just take over my education; she *attacked* it as if it were some giant monster that she was determined we were both going to overcome. So by the time I was ten I could quote from memory the first four books of the Old Testament and the first four books of the New. And some of the Psalms and Proverbs and parts of the epistles. The really remarkable thing is that I kept them all in my head. I had what the grown-ups called "a retentive memory."

Oh, yes, I was taught all about "the birds and the bees" too. And everything about "becoming a woman" and all the whats and hows and whys of sex. They taught me everything I should know. Well, no, actually they taught me more than I wanted to know. I always wanted to know about these mysterious things, but not very much.

And besides, in many ways I was far ahead of them and understood many things before they told me. For the Bible itself teaches all about these mysteries, and much better than people do. The trouble is people talk about it in whispers as if there were something wrong with it. The way I see it is that if God is in it, it must be all right. And I've learned by now that there are some things you can talk about and some things you just keep in your heart, except, of course, to talk to God about it.

"Fanny." It's Mama. "Are you all right?"

"I'm fine, Mama. I'll be down in a couple of minutes."

I walk around the room quickly feeling of everything in it. It's time to say good-bye, for I'm a young lady now—fifteen years old and, as it says in the Bible, it's time I "put away childish things." It seems like a thousand years ago and yet it seems like yesterday that God told me that happy days were ahead for me. And it has all come true.

For I, *Miss Frances Jane Crosby*, am going away to school!

Yes! There is a school for the blind in New York City and Mama made an application for me to be in it—and I was accepted! And this time I'm going, not on a sloop, but on a big steamer!

*God, this is the last time I'm going to talk to you in this room. Thanks again for letting me go away to school. I'm not the least bit scared. At least, I don't think so. Maybe I will be later, but right now I'm not.*

"Fanny?"

*Hold everything, Lord. I'll get back to you the very next chance I get. That probably won't be until I get on the boat. Don't leave me.*

By *Fanny Crosby*, July 15th, 1875

When thy cup is mixed with sorrow—
    Look beyond, look beyond!
There will come a bright tomorrow—
    Look beyond, look beyond!
O'er the darkest clouds of night
    Hope still hangs her beacon light;
Through the glass that faith doth lend,
    Ever trusting, look beyond!

When for higher pleasure pining—
    Look beyond, look beyond!
In thy Savior's arms reclining—
    Look beyond, look beyond!
Only He can know thy fears,
    Soothe thy heart and dry thy tears;
He, thy best and truest friend,
    Bids thee, trusting, look beyond!

Though thy dearest ties may sever—
    Look beyond, look beyond!
Parted here but not forever—
    Look beyond, look beyond!
From their bright celestial dome
    Heavenly voices call thee home,
While thy Brother and thy Friend
    Bids thee, trusting, look beyond!

# Chapter Seven

I am in school. I'm actually in school. I can hardly believe it. It's not like the school my sisters went to, where I could go occasionally and sit quietly and listen. This is a school especially for the blind where, if I have half the brains I think I have, I'm going to really learn something.

We left from Norwalk in a big steamer. Mama came with me. It was my second trip to New York seeking light. However, this time it wasn't physical light but the kind of light that would shine in my mind. And, of course, I have no doubt that this kind of light is going to make me live happily ever after.

What a change in New York from the way it was when I was here before. They have cars with steel wheels that fit into steel tracks that go right down the middle of the street. They call them streetcars and they are drawn by horses or mules. And anyone can get on them and ride. Anyone with the proper carfare, that is. And get off anywhere he pleases along the route. It's fantastic.

School is fantastic, too. It is all my fantasies come true. Mama stayed a couple of days and made all my guided tours with me through all the downstairs rooms where the dining room and classrooms are. And through all the hallways in the upstairs rooms where the students stay, and through the gardens outdoors where the school grows its own vegetables and fruit. And where there are benches and lawns and trees too. She led me upstairs and downstairs and round and round until I felt I knew every inch of it by heart.

For a few days I was lonely, and it took a while to get acquainted. I had to memorize voices, of course, so I could keep everybody straight. And I was homesick too, but not for long. The lessons were hard and strange and new. For though my head was crammed with tunes and poems and literature—Mrs. Hawley had read me just about every poem that had ever been written—it had very little in it of the things I had to learn here. Philosophy. History. Geography. Grammar. Political economy. Astronomy.

And worst of all, that monster arithmetic. They have metal slates with holes in them for that. It is horrible! I don't think I'm ever going to master it. I just don't have that kind of a mind. I even wrote a poem about it:

I loathe, despise, it makes me sick
To hear the word arithmetic.

But every other subject I loved. I caught on very quickly. My teachers found out from the start that I was very, very bright. Of course, I knew that already. I learned all about poetry, too. I learned how to parse and scan and write in different measures. It wasn't long before I was absolutely sure that I knew everything there was to know about poetry. In fact, there was no doubt in my mind that I was the brightest student in the entire school. No one ever came out and said so, but I could tell by my marks and I could tell by the way the teachers acted toward me. And besides, we had many famous people come visit the school and, every time they did, I was asked to write a poem for the occasion.

I think about this a great deal. I'm thinking about it even now as I sit in astronomy class. I can let my mind wander a bit in this one, as the teacher is going over stuff I already know. I'm going to be a teacher! That's what I want to do with my life. It comes to me in a flash. If I'm a teacher I shall make a salary and I'll be able to pay Mama back for all the money she has spent on me. And besides teachers have it a lot easier than students do. And they have a great deal of authority. They can tell other people what to do and I think I'm getting very good at that. I think—

"I would like to have Fanny Crosby come into my office for a few minutes." It's the voice of our superintendent, Mr. Jones. I didn't hear him come in, but I know his voice.

And then Miss Radcliffe says, "Yes, of course," to Mr. Jones, and then louder to me, "Fanny . . ."

But I am halfway to my feet.

"Will you go with Mr. Jones?"

"Yes, ma'am," I say.

I follow him out the door and down the hall and into his office.

He closes the door behind us and I walk over to the front of his desk and stand there respectfully.

"Sit down, Fanny," he says and takes ahold of my elbow. "I want to have a little talk with you."

He pushes a chair up gently to the back of my knees and I take ahold of the arm and sit down. Then he goes around behind his desk and sits there facing me. I like the smells in his office. He has a lot of plants in there and he has some flowers on his desk. The scents are all mixed up, so it must be a bouquet of mixed wild flowers. It has some red clover in there too. I can smell the clover.

"Yes, Mr. Jones," I say respectfully—but expectantly too. I know he's going to ask me to write a poem and I'm eager to know who the celebrity is who's coming to visit. I don't know how I could possibly say yes and squeeze this into my heavy schedule, but I shall try to be very kind and diplomatic if I have to refuse. Actually, it depends more or less on just who the celebrity is.

"Fanny," he says, "let me get right to the point. To begin with, your attempts at poetry"—he stops and clears his throat.

*My attempts at poetry?* I think. *Is that what he said? My* attempts *at poetry?*

"Yes, your attempts at poetry, Fanny," he says, reading my mind, "have made you a prominent figure here in the school. There are over a hundred students here and I dare say that you probably don't know all of them personally—only the ones in your own age group. But there isn't a student here at the school who doesn't know Fanny Crosby."

That would sound great except that I hardly hear it. My mind has ground to a halt at that "attempts at poetry" business.

"Now I'm going to give it to you straight, Fanny—the plain, unvarnished truth. And I'm not going to pull any punches. And you're not going to like it."

I stiffen. And then I force myself to relax again, for I remember that he can know as much about me as I know about him. We blind people can tell more about other people than they suspect. But it isn't all one-sided; they can tell about us too. And they have one advantage that we don't. They can see us purse our lips or scowl or stiffen or tighten up or all those other things we do that give us away. It's a sort of a language you speak with your body. I don't know what it's called. Someday somebody will probably have a name for it.

So I relax and fix my face in what I hope is a kind, respectful look.

"What I'm going to say is going to hurt, Fanny."

I nod, indicating that I can take it.

"But if you're wise you'll think about it and it may turn out to be the best advice you've ever heard. And I think you are wise, Fanny. I think you're a very wise young lady."

*You're not going to get me with that one*, I think. *I heard you the first time—attempts at poetry indeed.*

As yet, Fanny, you know very little about poetry. In fact, you know very little about anything."

*Oh, brother.*

"Very little—now listen to this, Fanny—very little compared to what there is to be known. My dear, you have almost all of it yet to learn. You haven't even begun. It's when we've learned just a little that we think we know everything. You don't know everything yet, Fanny. You're a long way from it. Now listen to me."

I wet my lips and strain a little forward in my chair. This is hurting.

"Your poems are good, Fanny, but they're not everything in your life. And the praise you get. That's not everything either. You have a good mind and I want you to use it. I want you to keep on storing it with knowledge—all the knowledge you can get. And think about what you can be— what God wants you to be, instead of thinking about how popular you are around here."

*Oh, golly, this is hurting, this is hurting.*

*Open your eyes wide. Everyone tells you that you have pretty eyes even though you can't see. And don't bite your lip,* I tell myself.

"Fanny—" he is leaning forward now. "Flattery and popularity are very fragile things on which to depend. The approval of people is great, but it's the approval of God that really matters."

I can feel the hot tears stinging my eyes. He is getting to me.

"Every good gift comes from God, Fanny. Your Bible tells you this. And that goes for your talents and your good mind. But, Fanny—"

My nose is running.

"It also goes for the food you eat and even the very air you breathe. It all comes from God."

I fish in my apron pocket for my handkerchief. I'm coming all unpasted. Something inside me is saying, *He's telling the truth, Fanny. He's telling the truth. I'm ambitious—and all in the wrong way. I've been living on flattery.*

"Fanny—"

*Oh, Lord,* I think. *Not any more, I can't take any more.*

*This pain is awful.*

But I guess he's through tearing me up, for his next words were words of advice.

"Shun flattery, Fanny. Shun it as you would shun a snake."

We sit in silence for a minute. He is waiting for me to say something. I pick up the pieces in my mind and try to put them back together. I take a long, deep breath and my words come out all wobbly. What I say surprises us both.

"Mr. Jones, you remind me of my father." Now why did I say that?

"But, Fanny, your father died when you were very young—too young to remember him."

"I know," I say, "and I haven't even thought about him for a long, long time, but I think—"

*Oh, good grief, I'm going to cry. This is terrible. I'm already down in the pits.* "Because," I begin. And my voice wobbles—bass, tenor, alto and soprano, as I struggle to keep from crying. "I think that's exactly what he would have said to me."

I get out of my chair and go around the desk and stand by his side. "And my grandpa, too," I say. My chest is heaving now. I feel as if there is a great weight on it. "My grandpa would have said that."

I put my hand on his shoulders. I wish I were a little girl again and could crawl up on his lap—somebody's lap—and cry my heart out, but I can't.

I take another deep breath instead. "Thank you, Mr. Jones," I manage to say. "Thank you over and over again." I kiss him on the forehead solemnly and with dignity.

"I'm sorry I had to hurt you, Fanny," he says.

"I know," I say. "But you've taught me a lesson I hope I'll never forget."

And I really mean it. He didn't let me dangle on my own, to learn it the hard way or maybe not ever learn it at all.

"Now I won't have to learn it the hard way," I say aloud. And I start for the door. He scrapes his chair back and takes me by the elbow and goes to the door with me. "You can go up to your room if you want to," he says as he opens the door. "I'll explain to Miss Allison. You can wait until lunch to come down, all right?"

"All right," I say, and my whole face bursts out into a grin now. I feel solemn, very solemn and somehow very happy all at the same time.

"Remember now," Mr. Jones says—somehow I know that he is grinning too, "shun flattery—"

"Like I would a snake," I say over my shoulder as I start down the hall.

# The Half I Cannot Tell

My heart is overflowing
　　With gratitude and praise,
To Him whose loving kindness
　　Has followed all my days;
To Him who gently leads me
　　By cool and quiet rills,
And with their balm of comfort
　　My thirsty spirit fills.

*Chorus:* I feign would tell the story,
　　　　And yet I know full well
　　　　The half was never, never
　　　　told—
　　　　The half I cannot tell.

Within the vale of blessing,
　　I walk beneath the light
Reflected from His glory,
　　That shines forever bright.
I feel His constant presence
　　Wherever I may be;
How manifold His goodness,
　　How rich His grace to me!

　　　　　　　　　　*Chorus.*

My heart is overflowing
　　With love and joy and song,
As if it heard an echo
　　From yonder ransomed throng;
Its every chord is vocal
　　With music's sweetest lay;
And to its home of sunshine
　　It longs to fly away.

　　　　　　　　　　*Chorus.*

# Chapter Eight

"Wee Willie?" my sister, Carrie, says. "*Wee Willie?* You actually call a student that to his face?"

"Of course, I do," I tell her.

"Does he mind?" my sister Julia wants to know.

"Noooo, he doesn't mind," I tell them. "His name is William. We speak of him as Wee Willie. Usually we call him Willie when we're actually talking to him. I don't think anybody's ever thought to call him Bill. If he were a little puny thing with a squeaky voice, we probably wouldn't call him Wee Willie. But he's strong and brawny with a voice like the bass notes on our organ. A chap like that could take up knitting or needlepoint or answer by any name or, in fact, do anything he wanted to."

"Tell us more," Carrie urges. "Tell us about all

of them. And about your teachers, too."

I am home on vacation and my sisters and my mama and Mrs. Hawley are gathered around me out on the big veranda and they are plying me with questions and hanging on every word of my answers. "Well, there's Miss Argyle," I say. "She keeps going up on her toes and back down on her heels as she stands and teaches. I can tell because her shoes squeak ever so little. Probably an ordinary person wouldn't even hear it, but I do."

"And then there's Emily," I say. "She's the first girl I met there. She was the first one to show me around. And then there's Angie and little Amy. They are ones I like the best. We're all in the same room and we help each other study."

"Tell us about the boys," Carrie says. "Do you know any cute boys?"

"Your poetry, Fanny," Mrs. Hawley interrupts. "Tell us more about your poetry."

I am relieved.

"Mr. Ogilvie teaches us our poetry," I say, "and he has a voice like a Shakespearean actor."

"But you have many great poets visiting the school," Mrs. Hawley persists. Number one, she is interested in poetry herself. And number two, she wants to get me off the subject of boys. "Didn't Longfellow visit the school one night?"

"Yes, and William Cullen Bryant. And Whittier! The poets most kids just study about in school and know only through their schoolbooks we get to see face to face—and talk to."

They ignore the face-to-face business. For some reason, people just don't know how to handle that one. They can't get it through their heads that we can "see."

"Do you know any cute boys?" Carrie persists.

"And Horace Greeley," Mama says. "We were so excited about Horace Greeley. Just to think—the great Horace Greeley—and my little daughter, Fanny Crosby!"

"Yes," I say, "I met him at a Christmas play. When I read some of my poems and he actually asked me to write some for his paper, I had to hang on to my chair for support. I could hardly believe it."

"Do you know what Grandpa did?" Julia says. "He was so excited about it, he walked four miles to get a paper that had a poem in it written by you."

"He never told me," I say, astonished.

"He didn't want you to get a swelled head," Julia says.

"No danger of that," Mama says proudly. I don't answer. I remember Mr. Jones; oh, how I remember Mr. Jones.

"Do you know any cute boys?" Carrie again!

"Carrie, for goodness sakes."

"Carrie, dear, please."

Julia and Mama both speak at once.

"Sure," I say. "There are lots of terrific boys there."

"But how would you know?" Julia blurts out. "You can't—" She stops suddenly. Mama has either kicked her in the ankle or given her a look that would squelch a stone gargoyle.

"I can't see," I say, finishing her sentence for her. "But we do have all our other senses. We're not allowed to really 'date' officially, but we've worked out our own system. Our favorite meeting place is in the chapel—the last place in the world the teachers would think of looking in the evening. And we have 'code tunes' on the piano. A few bars of music, or a chord. Or even a tune or a part of a tune played with one finger will do. Every couple knows its own signals."

Julia and Carrie squeal with delight. Mrs. Hawley sucks in her breath and Mama clucks. "And you get away with it?" she says.

"Well, we're either fooling the teachers," I say, "or they're letting us get away with it. I don't know which. Anyhow, it's working and it's fun."

Carrie and Julia are rolling on the floor with laughter.

I turn to Mama, "Did I leave anything out?"

New shrieks of laughter from my sisters at this.

"I mean about the school," I say, laughing too.

"No, Fanny," Mama manages after we've calmed down. "And you're telling it better than we could, Fanny. You see things that we don't." She reaches over and pats my arm.

"Fanny, you've changed," she says. "You're no longer the little country girl. You're a sophisticated world traveler actually."

"That's right," Mrs. Hawley says. "With all the famous people from all over the world visiting the school and with Fanny getting to meet them all and talk with them—it's almost being a world traveler. Fanny has become a learned young lady."

Carrie and Julia respond with little murmurs of assent and I sense a new respect, even awe, and maybe even a little twinge of envy in their voices.

"All the visitors don't come because I'm there. That's for sure," I say. "Actually they come because the school is state sponsored and it's an experimental school, too. It's one of the first schools for the blind in the whole United States. So they all come to see how it's doing."

But no matter how I try I cannot discourage what is beginning to amount to hero worship. I am famous and I'm stuck with it. It might have turned my head before that confab with Mr. Jones that day in his office. But I've had my head on straight ever since. I can just enjoy it now. And thank God for it. But I know now that I'm not the great poet, Fanny Crosby; I'm just a poor little blind girl who's hanging on to the Lord real tight and being hung on to just as tight by Him.

I hang on tightly because I am blind and because the river waves have sung me a secret.

Later when we are up in our room, safely tucked in bed, Carrie and Julia go at it again.

"Come on, Fanny, out with it. Do you have a boyfriend? What's he like? And do you have a signal? What is it?" I stifle a giggle. I sense their eagerness. They are about to hang on every word. They are aquiver to hear something spectacular. "He is a secret sweetheart," I say seriously. "I cannot tell you his name."

They catch their breath, waiting.

"And our tune is 'In the Gloaming,' 'In the gloaming, oh, my darling—' "

I leave them acquiver. In the ensuing silence, I can almost hear their imaginations running wild. I do not tell them that my secret "lover" is just old Willie, Sweet William, and there is absolutely nothing romantic between us. Once we fumbled into an awkward hug which left us feeling just foolish and sheepish. And that our "code tune" was not "In the gloaming, oh, my darling"—but a few notes of "Yankee Doodle."

No sense telling them that. It would spoil the fun.

I *was* tempted to tell them something else, though. There is a new student in the school. His name is Alex Van Alstyne. He is much older than me—maybe two or three years even. And everyone is absolutely mad about him. He is also much more advanced than any of us, and intends to go upstate to Union College Seminary in Schenectady when he leaves here. He's not only smart, but he has what people call a magnetic personality. And he's not the least bit stuck-up.

I get to talk to him once in a while, and he's so friendly, so *friendly* that sometimes I even get to thinking that maybe he likes me, I mean, *likes* me. But then he's just as friendly to everyone else.

Anyhow, I was tempted for a minute to tell my sisters about him, and maybe even make up something, like *we* met in the chapel. But I decided not to, because it would be a lie, and I'd be stuck with it later if they kept on asking me about him. Then I'd have to make up more stuff, when actually nothing is ever going to happen between us at all.

But I like him. I like him a great deal. More than I'd ever tell anybody.

Except maybe God.

On the way back to school Mama and I took a side trip to visit Grandma and Grandpa, and while we were there Grandpa took me on another side trip to see our old homestead where I was born and where I spent my early years. That's where we are now. Grandpa knows the people who live here and we are invited into the house.

How strange it all seems. The enormous rooms

that overwhelmed me before are actually rooms so tiny you can hardly turn around in them. The great distance to the barn is actually only a little way. And the creek, which had seemed to me like a raging stream, is just a little brook. Ned is gone and Dobbin is gone—long gone.

Before we leave, I stand for a minute and Grandpa waits patiently beside me. I take it all in, the meadow, the creek, the smells—the barn smells and the animal smells and the flower smells—all of them. I think of Wooley. I think of my golden summer.

"The doctor who treated your eyes, Fanny—" Grandpa interrupts my thoughts.

"I don't hate him anymore, Grandpa."

"I know. Anyhow, he left town. Nobody knows where he went. He said he would be sorry to his dying day. He has never forgiven himself."

"But I have forgiven him," I cry.

"I'm glad," Grandpa says.

"I haven't been angry with him for a long, long time."

"And your blindness?" Grandpa says.

I have to think about this a minute. "At first, I hated it," I say at last. "And then for a while I guess I just put up with it. But now I think that I can honestly say that I accept it."

"Just accept it?"

"That's as far as I can go, Gramp. Just accept it." There is a silence. Then—

"Hey, I hear you walked four miles to buy a paper to read my poem," I say, changing the subject. "You never let me know you were that impressed."

"I didn't want to turn your head, Fanny."

"It was probably very wise of you," I said. Then I tell him about that conversation with Mr. Jones in his office. I tell him everything, not sparing myself at all.

He takes my hand and squeezes it and we walk back up to the house.

I'm back in school now. I'm telling Emily and Amy and all the other girls all about my vacation. And they are telling me about theirs.

I have a hard time sorting out my feelings. For as much as I love my home and my family, and as great as it was to be with them, I'm still glad to leave them and to be back here in school.

*This is really my home,* I'm thinking as I listen to them all jabbering away at once about their vacations. I feel sorry for my sisters, for they can never *hear* the way I can. And even putting their eyes and ears together, I have a feeling that they can never *know* the way I can know. For no other sense can reach so far into the darkness as sound.

Sound is the great teller of tales.

# Happy As Happy Can Be

By *F. J. C.* Apr. 6th, 1881

Thy banner of love is o'er me,
   Thy righteousness covers my sin,
My banquet a feast of blessings,
   Refreshing my spirit within.

*Chorus:* Thus onward I go, rejoicing,
      And trusting, my Savior, in
      Thee,
      While all the long day I'm sing-
      ing,
      As happy as happy can be.

Thy banner of love is o'er me,
   I walk in its soul-cheering light,
That shines when my path is darkest,
   Like stars on the brow of the night.
                *Chorus.*

Thy banner of love is o'er me,
   My shield when the tempter is near;
Thy banner of love is o'er me,
   And so I have nothing to fear.
                *Chorus.*

Thy banner of love is o'er me,
   And when my life's journey shall
   close,
'Twill circle my head in glory,
   And wave o'er eternal repose.
                *Chorus.*

# Chapter Nine

"This is a very delicate operation," Emily says, "and must be carried out with the utmost precision. We cannot let it fail."

These words are met with a breathless silence. We are hanging on her every word.

"Now we've called only eight of you together for this mission," Emily goes on. "Any more than eight would be dangerous. There is too great a risk of leakage."

"And besides there wouldn't be enough to go around—" little Amy starts, but everyone shushes her.

"But do you really think we ought—" Jennifer says.

Everyone shushes her down too.

"This is no time to get cold feet," Emily says firmly. "It isn't that we don't have a part ownership in this thing, for we do."

And we all agree with murmurs of approval. All eight of us are in the room which four of us share. The other four have been invited by very careful selection, with the utmost secrecy and without the possibility of any slip-up.

"All right," Emily says, taking control. "Now, that that's settled, whom shall we send?"

Whom shall we send indeed. That's just like Emily. She's great at planning things and appointing other people to carry out the details. There's a little silence. I can feel it coming. It's the price one has to pay for being a leader. Sure enough.

"Fanny," they all cry almost in unison as if they had rehearsed it. I feel like Gideon.

"All right," I say. "I'll go, but someone must go with me in case I get in a bind. I don't know what I might run into." I turn toward Amy. "You," I say firmly. "You're small and quick on your feet." I can feel little Amy quivering with excitement over this great adventure.

And so we fall to, and carefully plan our strategy—just which door to sneak out of, the quickest way to get there, whom to avoid and whom to listen for. It was as if we were going to escape and venture forth into the dangerous streets of Brooklyn. Actually we were just planning to steal a watermelon.

The vegetable garden was a project of the whole school. Some of the teachers and all of the students had worked in it at one time or another all summer long, and the most coveted part of that entire garden was the watermelon patch. We had been looking forward for months to the time when we would reap the rewards of our labor.

But now the ugly rumor is spreading that these watermelons are going to be sold for the benefit of the school!

We decided that there was more than one way we could benefit. And that at least some of us should benefit more directly, namely, us. So now the time has come and we are about to put our plan into action.

"The important thing is the timing," Emily begins.

"Shhhhhh." I hold up my hands for silence though no one can see them. We hear two things at once—the clock striking downstairs and someone walking down the hall. "It's Miss Argyle," I whisper. "I can tell by her squeak."

Everyone shrinks back as if to make herself invisible. Much to everyone's horror, I spring for the door. I open it softly and step out into the hall and close it behind me. "Miss Argyle?" I say.

"Yes, Fanny," she says. "It's quite late. You should be getting ready for bed."

"We're getting ready now," I say quickly. I don't want her to come into the room. "Is it—is there—a moon out? I mean, is the moon out?" I giggle nervously.

"Yes," she said, "it's a beautiful moonlight night."

Oh, brother, just our luck. "I'll tell the girls. They'll be pleased to know," I say. Then I make my good nights and back into the room.

No one says a word. We listen to her footsteps going down the hall. We wait a few minutes. It seems like forever.

Then, finally, "She says it's moonlight," I whisper. "Come on, Amy, let's go."

We find our way easily—down the stairs, through the corridors and out the back door and around the corner, keeping to where we know the shadows are. At last we reach the garden. Every last one of us has rehearsed this at least a dozen times, for this adventurous plan has been abrewing in our minds ever since we heard the rumor that we were about to lose the coveted watermelons.

I creep along, one hand feeling ahead of me, the other hand behind me, feeling for Amy, making sure she is keeping close. I know exactly where the watermelons are, and I know exactly where the particular one I have chosen is resting—right at the edge of the patch by the path. I have already thumped it. I know it's ripe. In fact, I already deftly snapped it free of its stem only this afternoon.

I squat alongside it and Amy squats beside me. "This is the one," I hiss at her. I guide her hand to it and we both slide our forearms under it ready to hoist and run.

But wait. There are steps on the gravel a little distance away—stealthy steps. Someone is coming!

We both crouch, waiting, hardly daring to breathe. It is not just a rumor but a well-known fact that some boys have been plundering the neighborhood. Hearing the footsteps I wonder whether we should allow them to scare us off or whether we should attempt to scare *them* off. I don't relish either idea.

"Who's there?" Oh, glory, what a relief! It's our night watchman.

"It's Mr. Stevens," I hiss to Amy, as if she didn't already know. I put my hand on her head and squash her down so hard she grunts. Poor little Amy. I shall apologize to her later.

"Stay here. Don't move." I say to her in a voice to guarantee that she will stay frozen until further ordered. I straighten up and start down the path toward Mr. Stevens. I effect the most demure manner I can manage under the circumstances.

"Why, Mr. Stevens," I say. "What are you doing out here?" which is a pretty dumb question when you stop to think of it, but he doesn't seem to notice.

"I'm keeping an eye out for the boys," he says. "They're trying to steal the melons. They won't get by me. I'll catch 'em yet."

"Well, I should hope so, Mr. Stevens," I gasp, horrified that anybody should steal those melons. "But your voice sounds tired, Mr. Stevens. Don't you want to go in and rest a bit? I'll be glad to watch them for you."

"But, Miss Fanny—"

"Oh, it won't be any trouble at all, Mr. Stevens. I'm out for a walk anyway." Now, I do not for a moment expect him to fall for this, but incredibly he does. I take him by the hand and we walk back into the lounge on the first floor. I insist that he sit in an easy chair and put his head back and rest. I put my cool hand on his forehead. I don't know whether he is just humoring me or not. And it really doesn't matter, just so long as we get the job done.

I tiptoe back outdoors and whisper over my shoulder, "Don't worry, Mr. Stevens. If I see a single boy, I'll come arunning and let you know."

I hurry along the path back to Amy. "You'll have to carry it alone," I whisper. "Can you manage it?"

She tries to say yes, but it's just a gurgle. She is terrified. "Don't worry," I assure her. "Everything's under control. Here." And I squat and slip my arms underneath the huge melon and together we struggle to our feet. Then I shift the weight into her arms. She is standing there cradling a watermelon that seems to be as big as she is and trembling from head to foot.

"Don't be scared, Amy. The thing is as good as done. Just run back to the room as fast as you can and be quiet. Be careful. Listen for noises. You hear me?"

She doesn't wait for any more. She turns and flees. I look after her with my ears. In a minute both Amy and the melon are gone. I turn and walk back down the path. I walk slowly back and forth trying to gauge the time and listening for any sound that might indicate that those mischievous boys are around trying to steal melons. For some reason the thought escapes me that that is exactly what we have just done. I wait for what I think must be fifteen minutes and then go quietly into the lounge. Dear Mr. Stevens is about to doze off.

I tug at his sleeve lightly and he jumps and grunts and struggles to his feet.

"The boys didn't come around, Mr. Stevens," I tell him. "Not a single one. You had your rest. You can go back out now." He thanks me again and again.

"No trouble at all," I assure him. "I think I'll go back upstairs this way. I've had my—eh—walk. I'm done for the night." I hurry back upstairs through the inside corridor and get back to the room without meeting anyone.

The prized melon has already been dissected

with a kitchen knife, which Emily has snitched earlier and stored for the purpose. She even acquired napkins for us. Emily's ingenuity knows no bounds when she sets her mind to it.

We eat our spoils with muffled giggles and slurps and moans of delight. We spit our seeds into our napkins. We forego the pleasure of having a seed fight; if we started spitting seeds at each other we would never be able to collect the evidence afterward. The rinds are cut up in little pieces and wrapped in newspapers and stuffed into the bottom of the huge wastebasket. We pile our crumpled up paper and trash on top of it and hope for the best.

The guests we have invited to share in our mischief sneak back to their rooms and the rest of us, midst giggles and groans and bumping into each other in our excitement, attempt to settle down for the night.

Once in bed we stifle our giggling under our pillows. I, for one, can't stop giggling. I have more adrenalin in my blood than the rest of them, for I have risked more in this adventure in piracy.

I'm absolutely certain I'm never going to get to sleep tonight. What if someone saw us? We would have no way of knowing. What if one of the room cleaners slips on a stray seed tomorrow and the rest of them are discovered? What if Emily can't get the knife back to the kitchen?

But the sense of adventure is so great I cannot dwell on worrisome details for long. I fall asleep grinning, pleased with myself.

And the next day all eight of us go about grinning, sending little signals of secret delight to each other.

All day I am wondering just why I am so tickled. I finally figure it out. It's not the watermelon itself that's so important. It's the idea that people— especially our teachers—think of us as disadvantaged, people to lead around by the nose. It's just a bone-tickling experience to try to put something over on them—and succeed!

I put off talking to God about it for I suspect there is something about it that's wrong and I really don't want to put my finger on just *what*. Not yet anyway. I want to enjoy it for a while longer.

Tonight at supper Mr. Jones solemnly announces, just before dessert, that they are going to sell the watermelons and use the money for the school. A groan goes up over the whole dining room.

"But before we do," he says, and everyone is quiet, "before we do, we have decided to collect the choicest ones to serve for dessert tonight. Enjoy yourselves." He sits down amid much clapping.

I nudge Emily across the table. Amy, who is sitting next to me, kicks my ankle. I kick her back. When I get my watermelon I feel of it. It's a large piece. I cut into it with my fork. It's delicious. But not as delicious as that illegal piece we sneaked in last night.

Still I get a twinge. If God is trying to tell us anything, it's that we stole something He was about to give us anyway.

I'll think about it later. Right now I have an irresistible desire to giggle again.

It crosses my mind that maybe I could tell Alex Van Alstyne about it. I think he would enjoy it. But on the other hand, maybe he would think it was

terrible and not like me anymore.
I couldn't stand that.

# For Thy Glory

By *Fanny Crosby*, March 14, 1898

Only to live for Thy glory,
　　Only to know I am Thine,
Close to my heart like a treasure,
　　Clasping Thy promise divine;
Only to feel that in sorrow
　　Still Thou art caring for me;
Jesus, my blessed Redeemer,
　　This my petition shall be.

Only to live for Thy glory,
　　Only to wait at Thy throne,
Only to walk in Thy footsteps,
　　Led by the Spirit alone;
Only to glean with the reapers
　　Fruit of rejoicing in Thee;
Jesus, my blessed Redeemer,
　　This my petition shall be.

Only to live for Thy glory,
　　Bearing reproach for Thy name,
Willing to do or to suffer,
　　If at the last I may claim
One little place in the mansion
　　Thou art preparing for me:
Jesus, my blessed Redeemer,
　　This my petition shall be.

# Chapter Ten

"Fanny, there's something I want to talk to you about, and something I'm going to ask you to do— or rather, not to do, and you're not going to like it."

This doesn't surprise me for I walked into Mr. Jones's office with the feeling that whatever he said I wasn't going to like. It's hard to explain, but I get feelings about these things.

"Yes, sir," I say primly and remain standing. I'm a senior now—a senior in good standing, with most excellent marks and I haven't gotten cocky about it, at least not yet. I wait respectfully.

"It's about your poetry."

Oh, good grief, *that* again. I've been writing poetry like mad. It just seems to come flowing into my mind faster than I can memorize it or get someone to copy it down for me or, slower still, manage to copy it down myself.

"Yes, sir," I say again.

"Fanny, some people write rhymes because they are poetry *lovers*, not poets."

"Yes," I say politely. What I really mean is, *Get to the point, Mr. Jones. Get to the point.*

He clears his throat. "Well, I'm afraid you're getting sidetracked, Fanny, while you're preparing to be a teacher. Teaching is right around the corner for you. You're qualified to teach grammar, to teach rhetoric, to teach history—ancient history, modern history; you're going to be one of the most brilliant instructors in the institution. Why do you insist on wasting your time in poetry?"

"I—I have a witching sprite."

"A what?"

"A witching sprite, sir. She keeps tugging at me."

"Your sprite is a she?"

"Yes, sir, she's—eh—feminine gender. She creeps up to me at night and she invites me to take trips with her into the unknown."

"Fanny," he starts to interrupt, but I plow on. I am determined to finish.

"The name of my sprite is Poetry. She tugs away at my hand. She tugs at my hair. She tugs at my heartstrings. And she whispers to me, 'Fanny, Fanny, come with me—' "

There. I said it and I'm glad.

"Witching sprite indeed," he mutters to himself. But I have the feeling he is smiling. "Fanny," he says gently, "why, when you are so qualified in all these other areas, when you are so brilliant—why do you put such a strong emphasis on poetry as if it were your life's calling? Did someone tell you that this should be your lifework? Your grandfather perhaps?"

"No, sir," I say almost under my breath. "God told me." I stop. There is a silence. He is waiting for an explanation. "I was coming up on a boat from New York," I go on. It's painful now. I'm not at all sure whether I want to tell him or not. "I heard the waves," I say, and my voice goes up to a high tremolo. "I heard His voice. He said He had a job for me. I was very discouraged at the time."

"I see," he says, very gently this time, "and did He tell you, Fanny, that that job was to write poetry?"

This stops me in my tracks. I remember now. God hadn't said one word about poetry. He had just told me He had a job for me to do. I just shake my head miserably. I'm sorry now that I told him anything at all.

"This thing is very personal between me and the Lord," I say, almost in a whisper, as if I had imparted some great private secret and now wish I could take it back.

There is a silence. Then at last, "Fanny," he says, "this is the real reason I called you in. I'm going to ask you not to write any more poems—for three months."

This comes like a thunderclap. "Three months!"

"Yes, three months, Fanny. By that time you should be cured of this obsession."

He makes it sound like a disease.

"But I'm so sure that God told me that this would be my life's work, even if He didn't put it into words." My voice is trembling now. "May I please be excused?"

He says yes and I start for the door. I get my

hand on the knob and turn around to face him. "God has also taught me to obey those in authority over me," I say, my voice still trembling, "so, of course, I shall do as you say. I'll avoid poetry as I would avoid the measles."

I open the door and go out. He thinks I'm close to tears, that I'm going to cry because my heart is broken, but he's wrong. I'm close to anger is what I am. I go up to my room and fling myself down beside the bed.

*God, I'm not going to try to fool you because I know I can't. I am angry and I am frustrated and I think that the Soop is a very unreasonable man and he said some very hard things to me. He told me some people write hymns because they're poetry lovers, not because they're poets. No matter how you look at it, God, that was mean. He could have asked me not to write poetry for three months without putting me down like that. He didn't say one positive thing to me.* It comes into my mind that he did say I was highly qualified to teach and that I was very, very bright, but I ignore this. It gives me more satisfaction right now to stay angry, to feel abused. *I feel like Joseph must have felt when his brothers threw him in the well. And when Potiphar threw him into prison. He must have felt, "God, it's dark in here," and I know he asked you to get him out. Well, that's the way I feel. It's dark in here. Not just my sight. It's dark in here and it's going to stay dark for three months until I write a poem again and listen to my witching sprite. In Jesus' name. Amen. And, God—P.S. I don't like this one little bit.*

I get up from my knees totally frustrated. And sad to realize how presumptuous I have been to

God, how sassy.

But I feel bruised all over as if somebody had hit me.

Later I go through the supper hour in stoic silence, smiling bravely, my lips quivering a bit. I hope Mr. Jones is watching me. I hope he realizes what he has done to me. And I hope he can see how bravely I'm taking it. And I hope he's ashamed of himself! I intend to stay angry the whole three months.

But it is more difficult than I would have thought. In the first place, I have an incurably happy disposition which is not exactly an asset at a time like this.

In the second place, perhaps Superintendent Jones may be right. Well, *a little* right. My mind won't let him be *all* right.

As day after day goes by, I am more and more willing to concede that at least he meant well.

Besides, something happened last night out of the blue that was most extraordinary. Mr. Jones always makes announcements at the evening meal and they are always so great. I mean, you can practically count on the fact that some famous person is coming to visit or we're going to have a fun musical with a lot of guests invited. In fact, the only announcement I recall that made us all groan was when he announced they were going to sell the watermelons.

So, when he got our attention we all pricked up our ears, expecting something good, but we did not expect this. He announced that we were going to have a famous *phrenologist* at the school. He is a Dr. George Combe of Scotland. He had learned all about phrenology in Edinburgh when the great and famous Spurzheim was there.

While Mr. Jones was saying all this, we were digging each other in the ribs. And those who did not know were asking those who did know what on earth a phrenologist was.

"He can tell what your talents are by feeling the bumps of your head."

"You mean he's going to actually feel our heads?"

"Yes," I whispered, "your throbbing and distended heads," and I laughed aloud which was very much out of place, for after all I was going through one of the great trials of my life. I hadn't planned to laugh until my imprisonment was over. Actually, I wasn't too sure that I even believed in phrenology, but we discussed it up in our rooms that night and I found myself catching the excitement. I fell asleep wondering if I might be one of the lucky ones to be called up to put my head under his expert fingers.

That was last night.

Tonight I am sitting in the meeting in a state of expectancy that I try not to show. I pretend indifference to the whole thing. Only God knows what's whirling around in my head. What if—oh, what if he should discover that I am, after all, a poet.

I try to relax. Perhaps there's nothing to his phrenology after all. He might even be a fake.

I watch while Roy Fullenwider is called up to be examined. We all wait, breathless. And then— "Why, this boy is a mathematician," Dr. Combe says at last. "And no ordinary one either. He could do practically anything in mathematics."

We all sit up as one person, absolutely astonished. For the fact is that Roy Fullenwider can actually listen to two persons talking to him at the same time—and ask them to give him all the years, weeks, and months of their ages. Then he will inform both of them the number of seconds they are old. *Seconds.*

And as if this weren't phenomenal enough, he can do this while he is singing a song! And he is one of the youngest students! Now it would be pretty easy to thoroughly dislike a boy like this if he were conceited about it. But he isn't. He is the most happy-go-lucky and good-natured boy in the school. Mostly, I think we are proud of him because he is one of us. He is blind. This means a great deal to us, because so many people think that because a person is blind, he is also somehow not quite bright.

So when Dr. Combe felt of his head and declared almost at once that he is a brilliant mathematician, we were not only overjoyed but thoroughly convinced now that the phrenologist is indeed not only not a fake but a most accomplished man.

I sit here listening to all the exclamations of surprise and wonder around me. I am torn between my excitement and feelings of despair. What if I'm called up now and the great doctor tells me I'm good at history or grammar or something else and doesn't mention a word about being a poet? Now I hope I won't be called up. The disappointment would be too much to bear. I couldn't—

"Miss Fanny Crosby." It is Mr. Jones's voice. I slink in my seat. I think I'm going to die. Now I feel perfectly sure that I'm not a poet after all, that Mr. Jones will be right, and that I will never be able to live down my disgrace.

"Fanny Crosby?" It's Mr. Jones's voice, louder this time. I do not spring to my feet as I usually do (I am ordinarily a springer). In fact, those on either side of me *push* me to my feet, and in fear and trembling I walk to the front, sit on the stool in front of the great doctor and put my now-reluctant head under the scrutiny of his all-knowing fingers. I feel his fingers go through my curly hair and start to explore my bumpy scalp. I suddenly feel that my scalp is full of bumps—all negative. Surely now he is going to examine my bumps and sigh and exchange a long, sad look with all the teachers, and especially Mr. Jones. But instead—

"Why! Here is a poet!" I hear the long ohs and ahs of the entire student body and all the teachers. I can die happy now, I think, even if I am never allowed to write another verse. And then he goes on, "Give her every advantage that you possibly can. Let her read the best books. Let her converse with the best writers. This little lady is surely going to make her mark in the world."

Glory be!

I get up from my stool trembling. I make my way back to my seat. Those around me feel for my hands and grasp them in excitement. The evening goes on, but I scarcely hear another word that is said. I sit there shaking all over with joy. I know that Alex Van Alstyne is in the audience and I wonder what he thinks of *this*. But then I tell myself that he probably doesn't even care.

Tonight up in our rooms everybody else is shaking with joy and excitement too. Even the lady teachers drop in to share our excitement and to congratulate us, especially me.

And, of course, everybody there says the same

thing. They knew all along that I was a poet and a great one at that. Why he hadn't told us anything about me that everybody didn't already know. Everyone finally leaves and only those of us who occupy the room are left. But it is not the end of the excitement. We take off our clothes, folding them carefully, each in her own place. (When a group of blind girls share the same room there is no question of being messy. No one would dare. If you don't know where your own things are, you are out of luck. No one else in the room can find them for you.)

We take turns at the wash basins, washing ourselves and getting ourselves ready for the night. And one by one we crawl into bed. Then we take turns saying brief prayers, thanking God for the day and asking His protection for the night. After that, each one of us is on her own. It is a very special time for each of us has her own private time with God. This is an unspoken rule and seldom do we ever violate it. As mischievous and noisy as we might have been during the day, we are all careful about this.

I pull my covers up. I still can't wipe the grin off my face. And I'm filled with love. I'm filled with love for every girl who shares my room. I resist the impulse to get out of bed and go hug each one of them. I am filled with love for everybody in the world.

*God, I feel so happy tonight! Forgive me for feeling angry and frustrated before. I really am sorry. Sometimes I feel that I was a much better Christian when I was a little girl back on the farm. I trusted you for everything then. I haven't told you for a long, long time. And I want to tell you now. I accept the fact that I am blind. God, I totally accept it. And I hope I shall never, never be bitter about it again, not even a little bit. I have forgiven that doctor a long time ago—you know this. But now you have told me at last that I really am a poet. I know I am still going to be a teacher and I'm glad for this. I'm glad for anything I can do to help other blind students. The fact that I can still be a poet tickles me all over inside. God, I am happy inside and out. I'm smiling inside and out. Do you know how I feel? I am just filled with love, and especially love for you.*

I fall asleep on this. I fall asleep so happy that for a long time afterward I don't know how I ever *managed* to fall asleep.

This is the next day and it is still heady business. I awoke this morning in a state of excitement; it took me a moment to figure out why.

It's my bumps!

While I was sitting at breakfast, crossing my ankles tightly to keep from jumping, the Soop—Superintendent Jones, that is, made an unexpected announcement. He told us that we are to have a very important visitor tonight. No less than General Winfield Scott.

General Winfield Scott!

One of the most famous generals in the country. He was held in such high esteem it was even rumored that he might run for president. We were excited enough about this, but I was even more excited when right after breakfast Mr. Jones called me into his office. "Fanny," he said heartily, "here, have a seat."

But the best was yet to come. I had hardly gotten myself seated when he exclaimed, "Fanny, you may write all the poetry you want to and we will give you all the help we can."

I couldn't answer. I just sat there and quivered.

"And furthermore," he said, "you are now officially the poet laureate of the school. And what's more," he said, "tonight there will be several dignitaries of the town on the platform when General Winfield visits and you will be up there among them as our poet laureate. How do you like that?"

I was already so happy I could hardly stand it. This was almost too much. I could scarcely get through the day.

But at last, tonight is here and I'm seated up on the platform with all these important people and with the great general whom they tell me is at the very height of his fame and one of the most important dignitaries who has ever been in our school.

"Miss Crosby."

It is an alderman sitting next to me. I lean toward him. "Do you like a good joke?" he whispers.

"Oh, yes," I whisper back. "I'm always ready for a good joke."

"Then will you get up and pull General Scott's sword from his scabbard and hold it over his head."

I am too scandalized to answer.

"Come on," he says. "I'll get up with you and guide your hand to his scabbard and you can do the rest."

"I wouldn't dare," I whisper back.

"Come on," he says, "As soon as he's standing."

And in a moment, "Now. And I'm right with you."

He pushes me to my feet and before I scarcely know what I am doing, I am marching toward the great general. The alderman guides my hand towards the hilt of his scabbard. It's too late to turn back. I draw his mighty sword from its scabbard and lift it high above his head. I reach as high as I can for I have been told that he is well over six feet and I am scarcely five.

I am terrified. After all, I don't want to slice off his nose. You do the rest, the alderman had said. What rest? What was I to do now? It's too late to turn back. There's nothing to do now but carry on. "General Scott," I cry, "you are my prisoner."

What have I done? I think I'm going to die on the spot. But in a second the general's good-natured voice booms back at me. He laughs. "I surrender at discretion," he booms. "I always do, to the ladies."

Everyone is laughing and applauding. I'm about to sink to the floor. Then as the applause dies down he says graciously, "Here now, let me show you how to wield it." And he puts that huge hand over mine and we go through the motions of how to wield the sword. Everyone is laughing uncontrollably now. They are delighted. I let go of the sword, trembling so I can scarcely stand, and start to retreat, but he is not finished.

"Well, Miss Fanny," he booms, "I suppose the next I hear, someone will have picked you up and run off with you."

Everyone laughs again more loudly than ever. I should think of a good exit line but I don't have time to. It just comes out of me without even thinking. "Oh, no," I say. "Oh, no, Mr. General! *I'm* going to wait for the next president!"

The audience breaks into a roar now. The alderman grasps my arm and guides me back to my seat. I sit there, trembling. I can't believe I did this.

Back in my room I listen to all the excited chatter of my friends. I go to bed I think happier than I have ever been in all my life.

# I'll Praise My Redeemer

By *Fanny Crosby*, Mar. 20th, 1916

I'll praise my Redeemer as long as I live,
    His name my rejoicing shall be;
All honor and glory to Him will I give
    For what He accomplished for me.

*Chorus:* His banner of mercy is over my
            head,
        The cloud and the pillar I see;
        I'll praise my Redeemer and
            hallow His name
        For all His compassion to me.

I'll praise my Redeemer, the light of my
    soul,
    Who graciously heareth my call.
I'll praise Him, though billows like
    mountains may roll,
    For He is my refuge, my all.
                                *Chorus.*

I'll praise my Redeemer, my Savior and
    King,
    My precious Defender and Lord.
Forever and ever of Him would I sing,
    And rest on the arm of His word.
                                *Chorus.*

And when He shall call me from earth
    to depart,
    And soar to the arms of His love,
I'll praise my Redeemer, the strength of
    my heart,
    With all His dear children above.
                                *Chorus.*

# Chapter Eleven

"Wee Willie," I say, addressing him sternly, for I am a teacher now. He is foot taller than I; it is hard to look up at him and be stern. "Willie, I understand that you were assigned to show some visitors through the school."

"Yes, ma'am, Miss Crosby," he says respectfully.

Willie was an underclassman when I entered the school; I was only a little older than he. Now I am a teacher and he is a senior, but everyone still addresses him affectionately as Wee Willie.

"So," I continue. "And I understand that you gave them what must be considered a very impertinent answer. Will you tell me what it was?"

"Well, Miss Crosby," he says, "when I showed them the dining room, they asked me how blind people manage to find their way to their mouths when they're eating."

The corners of my mouth are turning up. I'm glad he can't see them. "And what did you tell them?" I say gravely.

"Well, Miss Crosby," he says, "I told them—I told them—well, I told them that we hitched one end of a string to the leg of our chair, and the other to our tongue—and by this means we manage to prevent the food from losing its way."

I'm having a hard time controlling my mirth by now. "You actually told them this?" I ask.

"Yes, ma'am, Miss Crosby. I did."

I really want to laugh aloud. How clever of him. *Ask a stupid question and you get a stupid answer,* I think, but I cannot tell him this. "But you realize, Willie," I say gravely, "that this is very impolite."

"But they actually believed me," he says. "They thought I really meant it."

At this point I allow myself a chuckle. I put my arms around him. "Willie," I say, "I know it was a very stupid question, but you must never be this impolite again. You understand?"

"Yes, Miss Crosby," he says gravely. "I do."

"You must remember this, Willie," I say, as I dismiss him. He knows I'm laughing with him. Blind people have a way of knowing these things. Besides I am in no mood to reprove anybody for anything.

For we were about to go to Congress. Yes, several of us. Some of our prize students—and some of the teachers—had been invited to go to speak to the Congress of the United States of America. And I was one of them!

A week later I am sitting on the platform—in Congress! I can't believe it!

And I, of all people, have been chosen to recite some of my poems!

And here in the audience is John Quincy Adams. And James Buchanan. And Andrew Johnson. And Stephen A. Douglas. And Jefferson Davis. And so many others. I cannot even begin to name them. Oh, yes, there's another name being bandied about here. I've never heard of him. His name is Abraham Lincoln.

I am absolutely petrified. I sit here in a trance before all these important men.

"And now, Miss Fannie Crosby." My knees wobble as I walk to the center of the platform and start my poems.

My voice sounds shrill and quivery. I try to remember that God is with me, that it is God who has given me this great opportunity. But I am scared out of my wits. Then it is as if God Himself takes hold of my hand and I just draw myself up to my whole four foot nine and my voice gets suddenly strong and goes up to the balconies and just fills the whole place.

When I am finished there is a great silence.

And *then* they burst into applause—and I can hear them rising to their feet in a standing ovation!

I am just carried outside myself with the ecstasy of it all. I start back to my seat and there are hands to guide me. And everyone is still standing and applauding!

Back in my room at the hotel, I am still all atingle over what has happened to me. I can scarcely believe it. I have actually spoken before both houses of Congress. And they have given me a standing ovation.

*God, I am still so excited I can hardly talk to you. I can still hardly believe what has just happened. You have been so good to me—far greater than I have ever deserved—but there is still one thing that confuses me. Well, two things. One is that I've written poems as quickly as they come into my head, but they don't seem to have any connection with what you told me that night on the boat. I have this feeling that all these poems have something to do with something but I don't know what it is.*

*The other thing is—Alex . . .*

The years have flown and Alex is back from seminary now, here at the school teaching music. With all his other training, his big thing is music. He is brilliant in it—a classical musician.

Now that we are both teachers we get to talk a great deal, and about more serious things. But we laugh a lot, too. We laugh about things that aren't even that funny. It's as if we laugh over nothing at all because we are so happy when we are together.

I tell God all this, although I know He already knows it. He knows my secret heart.

*. . . The other thing is Alex, God. He is my biggest problem. Well, no, I am my biggest problem. He arouses feelings in me that I've heard about and read about but never felt in myself before. Why, if we're just good friends, do my knees wobble whenever I am near him?*

# Gather the Children

By *Fanny Crosby*, Mar. 17th, 1893

Gather the children, dear Savior,
   Tenderly bring them to Thee;
Led by the voice of Thy Spirit,
   Grant that they early may be.

*Chorus:*  Gather them now, gather
        them now,
        Never to wander away;
        Into the fold of Thy mercy
        Gather the children today.

Gather the children, dear Savior,
   Into Thy pasture so fair;
Shield them secure from the tempter,
   Keep their young hearts (in) Thy
   care.
                     *Chorus.*

Gather the children, dear Savior,
   Teach them to honor Thy laws;
Then, with an earnest endeavor,
   Help them to work for Thy cause.
                     *Chorus.*

# Chapter Twelve

"Fanny, you wouldn't."

"Oh, yes, I would."

"You wouldn't dare."

"Uh-huh."

"But you can't."

"Well, you may be right there," I say. "Maybe I can't. I'm not at all sure I can pull it off. But I intend to try." We're talking about a problem with little David.

"I've just received a reply from his grandmother, Mr. Jones. And from the fat letter I think she's answered all my questions and then some."

I hold up the large envelope brought by special delivery. "If you can get somebody to read it to me and help me to memorize the information, I think I can pull this thing off."

"Fanny, you of all people should know that you

cannot fool a blind child."

"You're right, Mr. Jones. No one could have fooled me when I was six years old. I'm sure of it. No one ever did. But then I was never in a plight like David. He's hardly eaten in a couple of weeks. He has a temperature. He's so homesick that he's made himself physically ill. And if somebody doesn't do something, we're going to have to send him back home for his own health's sake. It's a desperate measure, I'll admit, but I'm a desperate woman. This child has got to get his education."

"Fanny, do you think for a minute he'll believe that—"

"He's going to believe, Mr. Jones, because he *wants* to believe. He's going to believe that I'm his grandmother because he so desperately needs to believe it. I feel sure of this. Let me at least have a try."

I hear him fumbling with papers on his desk. He's moving them around aimlessly trying to look busy. He's not fooling me for a minute.

"All right," he says at last. "I think you're crazy, but I'm going to let you try. I'll get Miss Palm to help you."

An hour later Adelle Palm and I are pouring over David's grandmother's packet of information. There is an incredible amount of material to memorize. Not only friends and relatives, but every animal on the farm is accounted for. Hens, chickens, lambs, cats, a pet dog, and every one has a name and every one has his own personality and behavior traits. And every one has a history. I've run the gamut of emotions—from mild doubts to total despair, but Adelle won't let me off the hook. "Come on," she keeps plodding me. "You started this. You were so blooming smart. Now prove yourself."

"His grandmother's older than I thought she'd be. And the list of pets and prejudices and projects and problems and personal preferences is prodigious," I say, popping the *p*s on purpose. Adelle laughs appreciatively, but actually, it's not funny. What if I should fail? At the thought of failure, I sigh and we get back to work again.

By the next afternoon I am at last ready. I had sent for one of her dresses and I have it on. It's a little big for me, but it will do. It has her particular scent of cologne on it and its particular tucks and ruffles will be familiar to the little chap. Her voice, she said, was high; I'll have to put a little huskiness in it so I can pretend I have a cold.

I go toward his room with fear and trembling, asking God to forgive me this deception. *Just file it under benevolent chicanery,* I tell Him. *If you want this poor, blind child to get his education then I've got to do this. You understand, don't you?*

I forget for a moment that I am talking to God who understands everything. But I am desperate.

Then a strange sort of a calm comes over me. I don't know whether it's God's peace or of my own making.

By this time I'm at David's door. It's now or never.

"David, David, it's Grandma come to see you!"

"Oh, Grandma, Grandma, I thought you'd never come." He rushes toward me, throws himself in my arms, nearly knocking me over. I back into a chair, feel for it, and sit down, drawing him close.

"Oh, Grandma, I thought you'd never come," he

keeps saying it over and over again. But finally, "And how is Shep?"

"Shep barked and followed my carriage all the way to the crossroads. My, he wanted to come. He seemed to know that I was coming to see you."

"Is he all right? Is he lonesome?"

"He's just fine, Davy, and he misses you. But he knows—dogs know these things about people they love—he knows that you're here to get an education so he doesn't mind waiting."

"And Skip, and Tabby, and my red wagon? And does my goat still get out that back fence?"

"Yes—Danny had to chase him clear to the south pasture last night. And there's nobody around to tip over the chickens' water now that you're gone." We both giggle. "Or snitch the apples on the special tree by the feed shed."

"Those apples are so great."

"They are good. It isn't that we don't want you to enjoy the apples, Davy. They just weren't ripe yet and we were afraid you'd get a bellyache."

"When you said I couldn't have them, remember what I did? I put a rope around a limb and stretched it to the upstairs shed window—"

"And made a pully and put the strawberry basket on it—" I've been doing my homework.

"And filled the basket with apples and I pulled them in, and it worked, too."

"It worked till I looked out the window and saw a basket going mysteriously through the air. I knew baskets couldn't fly so I investigated."

"And Father spanked me and sent me right to bed. Boy."

"Well, sometimes I think blind kids do mischievous things because they think they have to prove themselves." How well I know.

He is content now. He keeps patting me and feeling of my dress. He doesn't notice that it's several sizes too large for me. Everytime he starts to feel my face I grab his wrist and kiss his hand and mention something else I gleaned from his grandmother's letter. I explain to him that the best way to prove himself is to get an education and show the world just how smart a blind boy can really be. I mix this up with a lot of sweet talk and fondling and caressing and hair rumpling until it's supper time and his tray is brought in.

I motion for the matron to set it down and make signals to her not to give me away. The matron nods her head knowingly and explains to Davy what's on it. "My grandma will know what's on it," Davy says. But I tell him hastily that I'll miss my last coach home if I don't leave at once and that what's on the tray is absolutely delicious. And with a final hug and a promise to come back as soon as I possibly can, I make my escape.

A few days later I'm back again, fortified with another letter from his grandmother. I'm not afraid now, for the hoax is working! And besides, I tell myself, I can always fall back on "Oh, everything's about the same." And I can see he's getting better by leaps and bounds. So I can get away from his home news and wean him over to school news.

"Did you know that Grover Cleveland was here a few weeks ago to visit? And President Polk?"

"Grandma—the president?"

"So they tell me. Every person in the United States, practically, stops here to visit sooner or later."

Then I try something on for size, just to see if it will work. "I won't be able to come and see you next week, Davy, but I'll send you a nice letter and give you all the news from home."

"Well, all right, Grandma," he says finally. "And when you come I'll give you all the news of the school."

It's working, it's working. Glory be, it's working.

"Already I know some news, Grandma. Miss Crosby told me. Do you know that Jenny Lind is coming to visit us? She's the world-famous singer from Sweden. They call her the Swedish nightingale. And P.T. Barnum, the great circus man is coming with her."

And then he says something that makes me forget my role for a moment.

"Have you met Miss Crosby?"

"Oh my, yes," I say, trying to dredge up "Grandma's" voice. But it comes out like a croak.

"She's one of the nicest teachers, Grandma. And Mr. Van Alstyne. And, you know, Grandma, when they are together I can tell."

"You can tell what, dear?" I say. It's harder by the minute to keep up "Grandma's" voice.

"I can tell they like each other."

*Oh good grief. He knows. He knows what I have never dared to admit before. He knows I am in love with Alex.*

"What nonsense. Whatever makes you think such a thing?" I ask him.

"I can just tell. There are little 'waves' in the air when they are together. It's hard to explain. You don't understand these things, Grandma, because you're not blind, but blind people just *know* these things. And I can tell they like each other."

I suddenly discover that I'm about to miss my last ride home if I don't hurry. I beat a hasty retreat out of his room, closing the door behind me. In the hall I lean against the door.

My heart is pounding.

# Thine the Praise!

By *Fanny Crosby* Mar. 12th, 1891

Like the bird that sings at morning
   When it ushers in the day,
Thus my heart, to Thee uplifted,
   Sings aloud its grateful lay.

*Chorus:* O my Savior, through Thy
       Spirit
       Thou hast led me all my days;
       Thou hast crowned my life
       with mercy—
       Thine the glory, thine the
       praise!

Though the clouds may sometimes
   gather,
   And through storms my path may
be,
Yet I hear Thy voice above me,
   And thy ruling hand I see.
                *Chorus.*

When these fleeting scenes are ended,
   And to earth I bid farewell,
When I reach Thy blessed kingdom,
   Then in nobler strains I'll tell.
                *Chorus.*

# Chapter Thirteen

Probably at least five minutes have gone by and I'm still standing out in the hall, leaning against the closed door of David's room. I've managed to pull it off again. He still thinks I'm his grandmother.

But any sense of triumph or elation I might feel over my victory is swept away by that one horrible thought—he knows I'm in love with Alex.

I know only too well about the uncanny ability most blind people have to pick up vibrations like that. But David is only about six. If I am able to fool him into thinking I am his grandmother, how is he smart enough to figure out how I feel about Alex? Clearly, my feelings about Alex must not be just vibrating. They must be *clanging*.

It strikes me suddenly that this is the first time I have thought it in so many words. It's true. I *am* in love with Alex.

I finally find the power to move down the hall and start up the stairs to my room. I need to be alone with this. In the middle of the staircase I stop. What if there is someone up there who would stop me and want to talk? Anyone within three feet of me would guess my secret. I turn and go back downstairs again and down the hall toward the French doors that lead to the garden.

The garden. That's where I need to go. I need to be alone and think. I walk quickly down the long, gentle slope of the lawn. No, I *float* down the long slope of lawn—for my feet are scarcely touching the ground. I head toward a clump of trees to my favorite bench. It's an isolated spot. Away from everyone.

"Fanny."

It's Alex's voice.

I scoot under a low-hanging branch toward the bench and stand before him.

"How did you know?"

"Well," he says, drawling, patting the bench. I clear the few steps between us and sit down beside him. "Your shoes don't squeak," he goes on, "so you can't be Miss Argyle. And you're not muttering to yourself, so you're not Professor Albright. And you're not hesitant like someone who has been blind only a short time. You are fleet-of-foot, like one who has always been blind. You don't quite walk like someone who can see."

I am relieved that he is talking. It gives me time to catch my breath.

"You have a certain walk, Fanny," he goes on, "like you're walking out to meet life."

I still don't answer. I can't trust my voice.

"And besides," he says, uncrossing his long legs and stretching them out in front of him, "I smelled your cologne."

I try to laugh—my tinkling laugh that spreads merriment all over the place and says nothing too personal. But it gets stuck in my throat. I'm having a hard enough time just breathing, let alone laughing.

I'm trying not to read too much meaning into his words, but he has never spoken to me in a voice quite like this before. He knew it was I; he smelled my cologne; he knew my step. I am not like anyone else to him. I am special. The joy inside me spreads all over my whole body. I cannot laugh. It won't come out. I hang onto a slat in the bench so I won't rise right up into the air and fly away.

"I came out here to listen to the birds," he is saying. "Much of the music I compose I get from the birds, but I came out here to think, too. And mostly, everytime I'm not thinking about my work, I'm thinking about Fanny."

Now I know I'm going to fly. I hang on to the bench slat more tightly than ever.

"Fanny," he goes on, "Fanny with the dancing feet. Fanny with the laughing face. Fanny with the joy of the Lord in her very bones—"

Suddenly—without even realizing that I'm making the first physical gesture, I reach over and put my hand on top of his. He turns his hand around and clasps mine. "Surely, you've known all these months," he says. "Surely you've seen how much I love you."

He lifts my hand up to his lips and kisses it. From somewhere in the back of my mind comes the thought that he has used the words *seen*. I know what it means, so I use the word too. "And surely you have seen how much I love you too."

I'm still clasping his hand lightly, but it seems to me that I'm hanging on to it for dear life as if to never let him go. He uses his other arm now to draw me close.

"I've been asking God for this for a long time," he says.

"I've been asking it, too."

"Fanny with the little elfin face. Fanny with the curly hair—"

"You have never seen my face. You have never seen my hair."

"I am going to see them now."

He feels of my hair ever so gently, touching its curls. He feels my face with his fingers. I reach up with my other hand and explore his. He is every bit as beautiful as everyone says.

And then we find each other's lips. He kisses the corners of my lips at first, ever so softly. Then he covers my mouth with his. I move my lips under his, kissing him back. I am learning quickly.

It is true what I have always been told about blind people. What we lack in sight, God more than makes up for in all the other senses.

"My darling Fanny," he says a moment later, "we've got to make plans. We must be married as soon as possible."

"But we've had no courtship. We must have a courtship."

"Nonsense. We've had our courtship right here and now on this bench."

My wit, which had quite deserted me, comes back. I drag it back. "But you must propose—the way they do in novels. You must say, 'My dear Miss

Crosby, my long friendship with you has deepened into something greater. Miss Crosby—' "

"Miss Crosby," he says, and his voice is tender, "I love you more than I love my own life. Will you marry me?"

He is touching my curls again. This time he kisses them all over. And then my forehead. I think that if he ever gets down to my mouth I shall just slide under the bench and die. The ecstasy is spreading down, down, clear to my feet.

"Alex," I say, dragging up my wits again, demanding them to come back, "you've graduated from Union College. You've been to seminary. You are into classical music. And me? I just write simple verses."

"You're as sharp as a tack, Fanny, and you know it. Everyone knows it."

"Well, I have a very tidy mind."

"You're a genius and everyone knows it. We will balance each other, don't you see?"

"I've never really gotten the rough edges knocked off of me."

"I'll see to that. I promise."

We are being silly now, but only to avoid kissing each other again.

"Fanny, will you marry me?" he asks again. "I think—I know—that God has destined us for each other."

The moment he says the word "God"—the moment he says that name, the moment it is in the air, a holy hush is all around us. It is as if God Himself is right there with us, blessing us.

We get up from the bench, clasping hands, and walk slowly back up the slope of velvet lawn. The passion is gone now. It will come back later. We go back into the administration building to tell Superintendent Jones that we are going to be married.

*God, I can hardly believe what has just happened to me. Of course, I can hardly wait to tell Grandpa and Grandma and my mother, but I have to tell you first. I have always run to you first to tell you everything and I'm not telling you now anything you don't already know. God, I know that you promised in your Word that you would do "exceeding abundantly above all that we could ask or think." But God I have something new to tell you. I accept my blindness now, such as I have never accepted it before, and God, you know I love you. You know I've always loved you, but I have never loved you as much as I do right now. You have given me exceedingly more than I could ever ask or think.*

*And now you have given me Alex.*

# O Troubled Heart

By *Fanny Crosby*, Nov. 25/98

O troubled heart, why thus repine?
  Canst thou not trust His hand
  divine,
Who all thy life has been thy stay,
  And (led thee) gently day by day?

*Chorus:* O grieve Him not with anxious
      fears
      Of what may come in future
      years;
      In Him abide, be faithful still,
      And let Him lead thee where
      He will.

O troubled heart, why thus repine,
  If thou art His, and He is thine!
Then will He not for thee provide?
  What canst thou ask on earth
  beside?
                    *Chorus.*

O troubled heart, why thus repine,
  Though trials must—and will be
  thine?
With patient faith believe His word,
  And thou shalt reap a blest reward.
                    *Chorus.*

# Chapter Fourteen

"Miss Crosby, I really am too sick to get up."

It is little Teddy McMillan propped up in his bed. I cannot see him, but I know full well that he looks as healthy as a corn-fed hog ready for the fair. I sit on the edge of the bed and take his pulse.

"Isn't today the day of the orals?" I ask him as offhandedly as I can manage.

"Yes ma'am, but I really am sick and it has nothing to do with the orals." I don't answer. Let him sweat it out.

"I just happen to be sick on the day of the orals. Honestly, Miss Crosby."

I keep my hand on his pulse long after I've counted it. I don't know quite how to handle this, for I know he really is sick, but not physically.

For Teddy stammers.

Not in ordinary conversation nor at any other

time—only when he has to get up in front of the class and recite from memory what has been read to him the day before. I sit there on the edge of his bed and there's a long silence while I pretend to keep on counting his pulse.

"I think you have fortitude-itis," I say at last. "That's inflammation of the fortitude. In other words, there's something wrong with your backbone. Do you know what all this means, Teddy? Do you know what fortitude means?"

"Yeh, Miss Crosby. It means I got no guts."

"Well, you said it, Teddy. I didn't."

"Is that bad?"

"It's not good. It's apt to get chronic and *that's* bad. And it can get serious if it isn't caught and treated early. Do you know what I'm talking about?"

He emits a long, quivering sigh.

"Now I've told you the truth, Teddy, I'm going to ask you something and I want you to tell me the truth. Are you prepared for orals today? Do you know your piece?"

"Yes, ma'am, Miss Crosby, I do. I know it all in my head, but I know when I get up in front of the class I won't be able to say it."

"Teddy, I'm going to give it to you straight from the shoulder and I want you to listen real hard." I take a deep breath and plunge in. "Teddy, there is something that we blind people have to learn very early in life. We have to realize that we are not handicapped. We are perfectly normal people who happen to be blind. So we compensate for our blindness by developing our memories and all our other senses. But especially, our memories. And our memories are developed the same way our muscles are—by exercise. We have to keep at it. But, Teddy, you have a good memory—an excellent memory. I know this. And you have a good mind."

"Oh golly, Miss Crosby, I'm glad to hear this," he sighs with relief.

"Well, there's something else you've got to get into your head. We blind people are apt to blame any of our failures on our blindness. And it just isn't true. When 'seeing' people blunder or falter or stammer or whatever—they don't think so much about it. They just pick themselves up and go on. They keep on trying. But when blind people make a mistake, they blame it on their blindness. And this is what you're doing. And that's nonsense. When you're afraid, you can't remember what has been read to you, there's no way you can get a book and go back and read and learn it over. You have to remember it. It's the only way to go. And because you know you can't read it over, you're doubly afraid that you're going to forget it. And *that's* nonsense. You can always get somebody to read it to you again and, in time, you will remember it. That's the way you develop your memory. I had to do it."

"*You*, Miss Crosby?"

"Yes, me," I laugh. "I went through the same kinds of fear. And I just kept on trying over and over again. I was determined to develop my memory the way an athlete develops his muscles. I *trained*."

"Then it's not just because you're brighter than all the rest of us?"

"I guarantee you, Teddy. I am absolutely no brighter than anybody else. I just have a great memory because I trained it. And believe me, I've dissolved into tears more than once along the way. But I just kept on trying."

"But if I get up out of bed and go down to orals—what if I stammer?"

"Well, then, stammer. Just pick yourself up and keep on trying. And before you know it, that wretched stammering will go away and you won't even know where it went."

He laughs for the first time.

I suddenly think of something. "You know, I heard a story about a boy, and I know him today, but this happened when he was a student back in Harvard University. Why this chap—and oddly enough, his name was Teddy too. He wasn't blind and he wasn't afraid. In fact, he was pretty cocky—absolutely sure of himself. And one day in orals—I don't know what they called it at Harvard, but it was like orals—he got up in front of his class, confident as all get-out. For he was one of the brightest students in the class. And he began to recite a poem.

> At midnight in his lonely tent
> The Turk lay dreaming of the hour,
> When Greece her knee . . .

"And suddenly, his mind went blank. For the life of him, he couldn't think what came next. But he was undaunted. 'Greece her knee—' he said again and again 'Greece her knee—.' And everyone began to snicker. But he went on doggedly, 'Greece her knee—' and finally his professor called out, 'Greece her knee again, Theodore, and maybe she'll go and we can get on with it.'"

Both Teddy and I burst out laughing now.

"Greece her knee," he says at last. "Is it about greasing a lady's knee?"

"No-o-o-o," I say. "The poem is about the country Greece, and I suspect that line ended with 'When Greece her knee will bow.' "

"Oh-h-h," he says, laughing louder than ever.

"Do you know who this Teddy was?" I ask him, knowing that he doesn't know. "His name was Teddy Roosevelt, Theodore Roosevelt."

"Theodore Roosevelt? The president of the United States?"

"The very same."

We laugh again.

"Now," I say, "you can get up and get dressed and come down to orals class if you want to. If you don't show up I won't hold it against you. It will be our secret, just between us two. But if you decide to stay here I want you to think very hard of what I told you."

"Yes, ma'am, Miss Crosby."

At the door I turn. "Your only problem is fear, Teddy. Fear of failure. And you know God loves you and you know what you've learned from your Bible."

"Perfect love casteth out fear," he says triumphantly from his bed.

I close the door softly.

I tell Alex about it that night in our little house a few blocks from the institute.

"Fanny, you are a wonder," he says.

We've been married for over a year now and the ecstasy and the wonder of that day on the garden bench has not faded.

Our own little house! We have memorized every

square inch of it. It is the first time either of us has had a home of our very own and we have it together.

We laugh together. We talk together—there seems to be no end of the things we can talk about. We play together. We pray together.

And there are long times of silence too when each of us wants to be alone and we respect each other's privacy.

We argue together too—sometimes we have some pretty noisy disagreements—but oh, what fun it is to make up! Sometimes I even relish an argument just for the sheer joy of making up.

"You look at life through rose-colored glasses," he said in exasperation once during an argument; he forgot for the moment that neither of us could see. "That was singularly inappropriate, Mr. Van Alstyne," I answered with dignity, "in as much as I look at life through my other senses—mostly through my ears."

"Well, then, Miss Crosby, you look at life through rose-colored eardrums."

That was the end of the argument; we both burst out laughing.

He calls me Fanny with the laughing face. And although everyone else calls him Van, I still call him Alex, my beloved Alex.

Sometimes in the night I awaken and reach over to touch him to make sure he is really there.

But tonight, after our merriment over Teddy, we both fall silent. We are both thinking about the same thing.

A great pall of gloom has settled over practically the whole world. It started in India. And like a sleeping giant, it awakened and yawned and stretched its deadly fingers over all of Europe.

The dread disease of cholera!

We learned only a few weeks before that it had reached London and seventy thousand people died of it. We have been waiting for weeks, dreading that it might travel west and reach the United States.

"Fanny," Alex says and he clears his throat, "we have to talk about this."

I am silent, waiting.

"It could get over here, Fanny, on ships," he says.

I cross the room and kneel beside his chair. Vacation time is soon coming. We've planned to go upstate and visit our families.

"If it hits New York," he says, "they'll be sending the students home early. We'll take our vacation early and leave with them."

"But it hasn't hit New York yet," I say. "Let's not borrow trouble ahead. Let's trust in God. It might not happen."

But it did happen.

A ship from England landed at Staten Island. She was from La Havre. There were several cases aboard.

Then an immigrant ship arrived at New Orleans. They had already buried at sea seventeen who died of cholera.

It soon spread over all of New Orleans—thirty-five hundred deaths. New Orleans was a great center of travel. Ships left there going in all directions. They left clean, but on their journeys the dread cholera was discovered.

Meanwhile, the dreaded giant had poked its

fingers into New York.

Back at school, as I walk out of the room briskly—I know these halls so well—I run smack into something that bumps my shins. I reach down and feel.

It is a coffin.

I feel my way around it, not daring to question who's in it. I go down the stairs into the lower hall. I feel my way now for I know that there are more coffins there. I hear the cry of the truckman out in the street.

"Bring out your dead!"

*Oh, God,* I think, *they die so quickly, so quickly.*

Most of the students had been sent home, but the few who did not get away in time are trapped here.

Alex and I had a choice to leave, but we elected to stay. We are living at the institute now, working day and night. We tumble into bed exhausted to get what little sleep we can.

I stumble over more coffins down in the lower hall trying to keep out of the way of the men who are carrying them out. I am feeling wobbly.

Too wobbly.

I am having the first symptoms of cholera!

Not only have I taken care of patients, I have been helping Dr. Clements who is our physician at this time—making cholera pills. They are two-thirds calomel and one-third opium.

I find my way back to the room where Dr. Clements is working. I grab a pocketful.

I am perspiring. This is good. If I can only keep perspiring I'll be all right. With all my heart I want to go upstairs and crawl into bed and just die peacefully, but I know I must not. I must keep on exercising.

I hasten back to my patients at double speed. I must keep moving. I bend. I stoop. I prance into one room and out another. I run up and down the stairs. One part of my mind is saying, "You have cholera, Fanny," but the other part of my mind keeps saying, "You do not have cholera, Fanny." I absolutely refuse to believe that I have it.

*I absolutely refuse to die*, I keep saying to myself. *Not now. Not now. For I have a job to do and I know the certainty that I have not done it yet, that it is not finished. I won't die, I keep saying, and Alex won't die either. We can't. We're not finished yet.*

Finally, at six o'clock, I collapse into bed. I am bathed in perspiration. I don't even bother to wash. I'm too tired. I've taken so many of the pills that if cholera doesn't finish me off, they might manage to do so.

I drift off to sleep. I do not even know when Alex comes to bed. My last thought is a verse from the Bible that I know so well, "They that wait upon the Lord shall renew their strength; they shall mount up with wings as eagles."

I wake up in the night and realize that Alex is beside me. But I must not touch him. I crawl out of bed and make a bed for myself on the floor. I won't touch him. I dare not.

Within minutes the quilt I have laid on the floor is soaked with perspiration. Again the verse comes back to me, "They that wait upon the Lord shall renew their strength; they shall mount up with wings as eagles—"

I drift off into a dreamless sleep.

I awaken the next morning very early. It is still dark. I hear the cry.

"Bring out your dead!"

I sit up on my wet quilt. It is soaked right down through the carpet. And then I realize something.

I feel good.

All my old energy has somehow poured back into me. I get up and get out of my soaked clothes and strip myself naked. Alex is still asleep. I bathe myself from head to foot and get into fresh clothes. I roll up the quilt and my soaked clothes and roll them out into the hall to be carried away to the laundry. I kiss Alex ever so lightly so as not to awaken him. I go downstairs to the dining room where the few of us who are left are having breakfast.

I am hungry. I am actually hungry! I feel all new again!

Those who have been on duty are ready to go to bed. Those of us who have slept are ready to begin again. We have our morning prayers together and I go back on duty with a vengeance, with a strength I have not known in many weeks.

When the truckman goes by our institution again and cries out, "Bring out your dead," there will be no more coffins from this house. I feel sure of this.

But I feel sure of this too—the great giant cholera will yawn and lie down and go back to sleep again. It may take a few weeks, even months, but he surely will.

I trip back upstairs to awaken Alex.

I am Fanny with a laughing face again. For it

will come, it will come. The institute will be ring-
ing with laughter again! But I shall never be able
to forget the cry of the truckman out in the street,
"Bring out your dead."

I shall hear it in my heart for the rest of my life.

# My Heart and My Treasure are There

### By *Fanny Crosby*, Apr. 14th, 1893

Away in the beautiful home of the
blest,
  Beyond the dark shadows of care,
Where sorrow is lost in the transport of
rest,
  My heart and my treasures are
  there.

*Chorus:* By faith I behold the city of
gold,
    Its portals wide open that
    stand;
    O, there shall I sing at the feet
    of my King,
    And dwell in Immanuel's
    land.

Away in the beautiful home of the
blest,
  Whose skies are so lovely and fair,
Where all in the verdure of summer is
dressed,
  Sweet voices are calling me there.
                                    *Chorus.*

Away in the beautiful home of the soul,
  Where crowns of rejoicing they wear;
I thirst for the fountains of pleasure
that roll,
  What joy, O what joy to be there.
                                    *Chorus.*

# Chapter Fifteen

"Fanny, your publisher sent over the proofs for your latest book. Mr. Jones wants to see you in his office as soon as you can manage it."

I grab the proofs and hurry into the Soop's office.

"Fanny, sit down," he says and hurries to pull up a chair for me.

"Thank you, but I can't stay. I've started a poem for Daniel Webster and I must finish it. It has to be in tomorrow morning's paper. Poor dear Mr. Webster. He's dead. This is what I've written so far:

A casket has broken—a jewel has fled—
The mighty has fallen—the peerless is dead!
And the heart of the nation is bleeding once more

For her eagle lies low on her desolate shore!

"That's as far as I got."

"Fanny, don't go any further. Daniel Webster isn't dead. It was a hoax to sell papers. I just heard of it."

"Isn't dead? Daniel Webster isn't dead?"

"Fanny, you look disappointed. Shame on you."

"Well, it was an oversight on his part not to die. This is a pretty stirring poem. My little witching sprite will be disappointed."

"Your little witching sprite is doing all right. Your sheet music is sweeping the country. You're getting to be famous."

"Oh, I haven't done that much."

"Nonsense. Don't be so modest, Fanny. Your 'Prairie Flower' is on the best-seller list and there's your 'Glad to Get Home' and 'There's Music in the Air' and your 'Flower Queen.'—

He's run out of titles. He pauses for a minute and then, "And I'm the man who tried to discourage you from writing poetry."

"Oh, well," I say, "a prophet is not without honor—except in a Soop's office."

At the door I turn. "I didn't mean to be so flip over Daniel Webster. It's because I was so relieved to find he wasn't dead."

"You don't have to explain, Fanny. I know how dearly you love him."

I find my way to the music room to see if Alex has any free time. He is there and not busy. I hand him my little bundle of proofs proudly.

"Galleys from my new book came this morning." I always hand him the galleys for each new book as if I were presenting him with a child. One of the great joys of my life is that he is so immensely proud of me.

"Is this one under your own name—Fanny Crosby?" he asks.

"I promised, Alex, I wouldn't fool you. I'll use my own name."

It was an old argument. I had wanted to write under the name of Mrs. Van Alstyne and Alex had protested.

"But I am your wife, Alex," I had said. "We are one."

"We are one," he insisted, "and we are also two. We are individual people, and neither one of us is going to swallow the other one up. You will always be Fanny Crosby." He hands the galleys back to me. "Of course, you can be my wife too—on the side."

"I am your wife *first*," I remind him solemnly, "and don't you forget it."

He finds my nose and kisses me on the end of it.

I leave him then and go off to find someone who has a free period and can read my galleys to me.

Maybe that's the secret. Maybe that's why our marriage is so great. We are totally wrapped up in each other in one sense, and yet each of us has managed to keep on being a person in his own right. Neither one of us smothers the other. Alex is proud of me, and he is so charming and popular with everyone at the school and everybody in our wider circle of friends outside, and I am so proud of him I can hardly stand it.

As I find my way down the hall, I'm as happy as any author could be on the day the galleys come back. And as any wife can be who has just been kissed and stirred by her husband. My life seems to be all in shining pieces, in bright and beautiful color. I have the strangest feeling that something is going to happen to pull all these pieces together.

I'm dreaming.

No, it's more than a dream. It's more a feeling of reality, for all my senses are completely alive and awake. My body is asleep. I don't know how I know this, but I do. I'm in an immense observatory and in front of me is an absolutely enormous telescope. Bigger than any telescope I had ever even imagined, and I can see everything clearly. All my life in my most vivid dreams, my sight has appeared to be fully restored. I dream in full color. But this is more vivid—the most vivid sense of reality that I have ever known in any dream.

Suddenly I realize there is a guide standing beside me. I don't know who he is, but he points. And I look and see a very bright star that seems to beckon me. I am drawn toward this one star. I go past all the other stars. I go past the scenery, such as I have never had described to me on earth before. There are no words to express it. It is so beautiful.

At last we come to a river and we stop, my guide and I.

"Can't we go on?" I ask him.

"Not now, Fanny," he says. "You must go back to earth and do your work there before you can come back here."

A feeling of immeasurable sadness comes over me.

"Don't be sad, Fanny, I'll open the gates a little bit so you can hear some of the music."

I stand there absolutely transfixed. I am lifted right out of myself. I hear music such as I never dreamed even existed. It is beyond anything my senses can handle.

"I can't handle this!" Did I cry out? Or did it just explode inside me?

Now I'm up on my elbows in bed. The vivid picture is gone. The music is gone. An indescribable peace has settled over me.

I lie back on my pillows and stare up into the darkness. I must hug this very close to my heart. It seems to me a very private thing I cannot share. At least for a while, except with Alex. In the next few days I cannot shake off the feeling of anticipation.

"Mr. Bradbury, I'd like you to meet Mr. and Mrs. Van Alstyne."

"Ah, yes," Alex says, "we've heard of you. You are a hymn writer of considerable fame. My wife you would know better as Fanny Crosby. She knows everybody."

"We both know everybody," I say laughing. And it is true. Our social life is one round of socials and musicals and soirees. God has surely cast our lines in pleasant places.

I had been wanting to meet the famous Mr. William Bradbury for years. We are off by ourselves in a little group. There will be a musical later, but right now the guests are just socializing.

"Mrs. Van Alstyne, I've been wanting to meet you for years."

This startles me. It is exactly what I have just been thinking. For a minute I don't know whether he said it or I said it.

"For many years," he goes on, "I've been wanting you to write for me. Somehow I've never gotten the opportunity to talk to you about it."

Yes, he said it all right.

Now he's plunging into an animated conversation about the merger of the famous hymn writer William Bradbury—and a little blind woman named Fanny Crosby.

As I lie in bed, I'm still in a daze. Not over the merger, but over the way this merger pulled all the scattered pieces of my whole life together. The merger is the missing piece.

"The merger is the missing piece, Alex," I say aloud.

"The missing piece?"

"Yes, way back when I was a child, I asked God to give me a job to do. And He promised that He would, but He never told me what it was. And then He gave me the desire to write poems. And then He gave me you, my darling. That was the best of all. But then I began to write *secular* songs by the bushel."

"By the barrel."

"Well, yes, then, by the barrel. Then He gave me that wonderful dream only a week ago, but now, at last—He has told me exactly what He wants to do. He wants me to write hymns. Why didn't I see it before?"

"You are dim-witted, Fanny, my love."

We both laugh for sheer joy as he pulls my head over to rest on his shoulder.

It is far into the night now. Alex has gone to sleep. But I am too excited to sleep. I think of that beautiful dream again. And I write my very first hymn for Mr. Bradbury.

> We are going, we are going,
> To a home beyond the skies,
> Where the roses never wither,
> And the sunlight never dies.

Then my mind keeps racing. It won't stop. And I think of the little girl in the boat who asked God for a job to do and asked Him not to pass her by.

> Pass me not, O gentle Savior
> Hear my humble cry;
> While on others Thou are calling,
> Do not pass me by . . .

*God, if people ever do sing this hymn, they'll think I'm crazy to suggest that you will ever pass anybody by, but you know what I know. And you know what I mean.*

I don't remember if I said anything else to God. I drifted off to sleep.

My real mission has begun.

# Chapter Sixteen

A little old carriage pulls up in front of a little old house on a little old street in Brooklyn—and a little old lady gets out. She says a gay farewell to the folks in the carriage, declines their offer of help, gets out by herself and goes up the steps to the front door. The carriage goes on as she lets herself in and closes the door behind her. I know that little old lady. I know her well. I have known her for a long, long time. For that little old lady is I.

I have just described myself—as if I were someone else looking at me. I have no idea what I look like. I can't see myself.

I can *feel* me. My waist is still as tiny as the day I was married. My step is still as sure. My spirit is still as young.

I *feel* young.

I am in my eighties.

I hope I am still "Fanny with the laughing face."

Alex always called me that. And I hope I still look at life "through rose-colored eardrums," as he used to say.

"Alex?" I want to call out when I get inside. I want to call that every time I go into our little house.

But Alex isn't here.

I take off my hat and gloves.

Before I can do anything else the big brass knocker knocks on the front door. I open the door.

"Miss Crosby?"

"Yes."

"I'm Willie—Wee Willie. Do you remember me?" And he gives me his full name, although I do not need it.

"Willie," I cry. "Wee Willie. Can it really be you? Come in. Come *in!*"

He comes in and he starts to shake hands, but instead we fall into each others arms, laughing. For he is the naughty boy who told the visitors that we found our way to our mouths by tying a string to our tongues and the other to the leg of a chair.

"Oh, you were a naughty, wretched boy," I say. "But how I loved you."

I draw him into the living room and we sit down.

"I've loved you all my life, Miss Crosby."

"Don't call me Miss Crosby. Call me Fanny."

"But you are so famous now."

"I'll settle for Miss Fanny. That's as far as I can go."

"I'm sorry to hear about Mr. Van Alstyne," he says at last.

My mind goes crashing back.

The year of illness. The year the institute cut down on my classes so that I could stay home most of the time and nurse him.

The night he died in my arms.

It was night for me, but it was morning for him.

He had gone beyond that star and into that gate that had been opened only a few inches for me. He was hearing the indescribably beautiful music that I had been allowed to hear only for a few minutes.

"But he can see now, Willie. And do you know the very first person he saw?"

He fumbles for a handkerchief.

"The first person he saw was Jesus."

We both dab at our eyes, but not in sorrow. We are overcome by something else and neither of us can put it into words.

"Are you going to continue to live here alone?" he says at last.

"Well, I've lived here awhile without him, but now my sister is coming for me. I am to go back to Bridgeport to live with her."

"Not to retire, Miss Fanny, and disappear from our lives."

"Oh, no," I say. "I'm going to continue to lecture and to write hymns and to—to gather sheaves until the sun goes down."

"You've written so many hymns. How many have you written?"

"Oh, thousands. I've lost count. My last count was, well, at least over five thousand, I guess. My only regret is that I had no control over which hymns were published and which were not. That was the job of the publishers. And as I look back I think that many of the really good ones were left out and some of the weaker ones were published. This grieves me. But I can do nothing about it. One thing I can say, Willie, God has led me every step of the way. He has given me a life beyond anything I had ever dreamed. Do you know, Willie, that—except for Washington—I have known personally every president of the United States?"

We chat for a while and finally he leaves, but what I have said sticks in my mind.

God has led me every step of the way.

I go back into the living room and sit down. I punch my fists into my face hard. I must get this down in my mind.

All the way my Savior leads me . . .

I finish the hymn. I hope I can keep it in my mind. I must keep it in my mind until I can get someone to copy it down. For it is true.

All the way my Savior has led—all the way.

Tomorrow my sister will come for me. She will stay awhile and we will have all sorts of gay farewell parties at the institute. There are parties planned all over town. I have so many friends I cannot begin to count them all. And they have all sorts of things planned for me before I leave. We have, I think, at least a couple of weeks of this. And she will be dazzled at the people I know. It will be such fun—such a gay time—

But I will never know this house again.

I go up the stairs feeling the bannister. Why, we have worn a groove in this bannister, going up and coming down. Alex and I have put our stamp on this little house.

I sit down on the top step and survey the down-stairs for all the world as if I could see. Before I leave here I shall go around on the last day and touch everything in it and say good-bye.

And I shall go down to the cemetery as I have done every day and touch the sod over Alex's grave. And tell him where I'm going. I know he is not there in the grave, but with the Lord. But it comforts me to do this and God understands.

What a joy my life has been. No—is being. Because I'm far from finished yet.

*God, I must not, I cannot be sad about anything. I miss Alex, but you gave me forty-five years of him. And practically every moment of them were happy. You allowed me to write all those hymns and, like it says in the Bible, you've caused me to stand before kings. I can find nothing but thanks in my heart. There has not failed one word of all your good promise. I'm going to keep on fulfilling my part of that promise right up to the end. There's a lot of life in the little old blind lady yet!*

*About being blind, Lord, there is something else I must tell you. At first I had a hard time dealing with it. And then I learned to accept it. And now something even better has happened.*

*I thank you for it!*

*I can see now how all the pieces of my life have fit together. And blindness was a part of the whole thing. I shall keep on thanking you for the rest of my life and I shall write hymns until the day comes when that door will be open all the way for me. And on that golden morning, the first One I shall see—is you.*

*God, I think we have another hymn on our hands. It's forming in my mind. I'm going to call it—"And I Shall See Him Face to Face."*

# A Wonderful Saviour Is Jesus My Lord

Fanny J. Crosby, 1890

William J. Kirkpatrick, 1890

1. A won-der-ful Sav-ior is Je-sus my Lord, A won-der-ful
2. A won-der-ful Sav-ior is Je-sus my Lord, He tak-eth my
3. With num-ber-less bless-ings each mo-ment He crowns, And, filled with His
4. When clothed in His bright-ness, trans-port-ed I rise To meet Him in

Sav-ior to me; He hid-eth my soul in the cleft of the rock, Where
bur-den a-way; He hold-eth me up, and I shall not be moved, He
full-ness di-vine, I sing in my rap-ture, O glo-ry to God For
clouds of the sky, His per-fect sal-va-tion, His won-der-ful love, I'll

*Refrain*

riv-ers of pleas-ure I see.
giv-eth me strength as my day.    He hid-eth my soul in the cleft of the rock
such a Re-deem-er as mine!
shout with the mil-lions on high.

That shad-ows a dry, thirst-y land; He hid-eth my life in the depths of His love,

And cov-ers me there with His hand, And cov-ers me there with His hand.

# All the Way My Saviour Leads Me

Fanny J. Crosby. 1875

Robert Lowry. 1875

1. All the way my Sav-ior leads me; What have I to ask be-side?
2. All the way my Sav-ior leads me; Cheers each wind-ing path I tread;
3. All the way my Sav-ior leads me; O the full-ness of His love!

Can I doubt His ten-der mer-cy, Who through life has been my guide?
Gives me grace for ev-ery tri-al, Feeds me with the liv-ing bread;
Per-fect rest to me is prom-ised In my Fa-ther's house a-bove;

Heav'n-ly peace, di-vin-est com-fort, Here by faith in Him to dwell!
Though my wea-ry steps may fal-ter, And my soul a-thirst may be,
When my spir-it, clothed im-mor-tal, Wings its flight to realms of day,

For I know, what-e'er be-fall me, Je-sus do-eth all things well;
Gush-ing from the rock be-fore me, Lo! a spring of joy I see,
This my song through end-less a-ges, Je-sus led me all the way.

For I know, what-e'er be-fall me, Je-sus do-eth all things well.
Gush-ing from the rock be-fore me, Lo! a spring of joy I see.
This my song through end-less a-ges, Je-sus led me all the way.

# Blessed Assurance, Jesus Is Mine

Fanny J. Crosby, 1873

Phoebe P. Knapp, 1873

1. Bless-ed as-sur-ance, Je-sus is mine! O, what a fore-taste of
glo-ry di-vine! Heir of sal-va-tion, pur-chase of God,
Born of His Spir-it, washed in His blood.

2. Per-fect sub-mis-sion, per-fect de-light, Vi-sions of rap-ture now
burst on my sight; An-gels de-scend-ing, bring from a-bove
Ech-oes of mer-cy, whis-pers of love.

3. Per-fect sub-mis-sion, all is at rest, I in my Sav-ior am
hap-py and blest; Watch-ing and wait-ing, look-ing a-bove,
Filled with His good-ness, lost in His love.

*Refrain*

This is my sto-ry, this is my song, Prais-ing my Sav-ior all the day long; This is my sto-ry, this is my song, Prais-ing my Sav-ior all the day long.

# He Hideth My Soul

Words, Fanny J. Crosby, 1890.                    William J. Kirkpatrick, 1890.

1. A wonderful Savior is Jesus my Lord, A wonderful Savior to me; He hideth my soul in the *cleft of the rock, Where rivers of pleasure I see.
2. A wonderful Savior is Jesus my Lord, He taketh my burden away; He holdeth me up, and I shall not be moved, He giveth me strength as my day.
3. With numberless blessings each moment he crowns, And filled with his fullness divine, I sing in my rapture, oh, glory to God For such a Redeemer as mine!
4. When clothed in his brightness, transported I rise To meet him in clouds of the sky, His perfect salvation, his wonderful love I'll shout with the millions on high.

He hideth my soul in the cleft of the rock That shadows a dry, thirsty land; He hideth my life in the depths of his love, And covers me there with his hand, And covers me there with his hand.

*Exodus 33:22.

# I Am Thine, O Lord

Fanny J. Crosby, 1875

William H. Doane, 1875

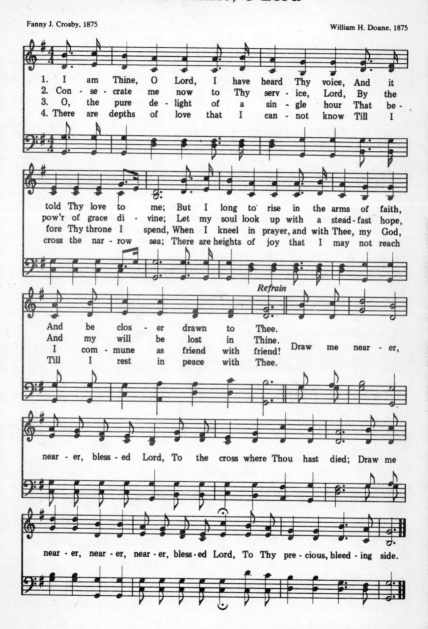

1. I am Thine, O Lord, I have heard Thy voice, And it
2. Con - se - crate me now to Thy serv - ice, Lord, By the
3. O, the pure de - light of a sin - gle hour That be -
4. There are depths of love that I can - not know Till I

told Thy love to me; But I long to rise in the arms of faith,
pow'r of grace di - vine; Let my soul look up with a stead - fast hope,
fore Thy throne I spend, When I kneel in prayer, and with Thee, my God,
cross the nar - row sea; There are heights of joy that I may not reach

*Refrain*

And be clos - er drawn to Thee.
And my will be lost in Thine. Draw me near - er,
I com - mune as friend with friend!
Till I rest in peace with Thee.

near - er, bless - ed Lord, To the cross where Thou hast died; Draw me

near - er, near - er, near - er, bless - ed Lord, To Thy pre - cious, bleed - ing side.

# Jesus Is Tenderly Calling You Home

Fanny J. Crosby, 1883

George C. Stebbins, 1883

# Jesus, Keep Me Near the Cross

Fanny J. Crosby, 1869

William H. Doane, 1869

1. Je - sus, keep me near the cross, There a pre - cious foun - tain
2. Near the cross, a trem - bling soul, Love and mer - cy found me;
3. Near the cross! O Lamb of God, Bring its scenes be - fore me;
4. Near the cross I'll watch and wait, Hop - ing, trust - ing ev - er,

Free to all, a heal - ing stream, Flows from Cal - v'ry's moun - tain.
There the Bright and Morn - ing Star Sheds its beams a - round me.
Help me walk from day to day With its shad - ows o'er me.
Till I reach the gold - en strand Just be - yond the riv - er.

*Refrain*

In the cross, in the cross Be my glo - ry ev - er;

Till my rap - tured soul shall find Rest be - yond the riv - er.

# More Like Jesus Would I Be

Fanny J. Crosby, 1867

William H. Doane, 1867

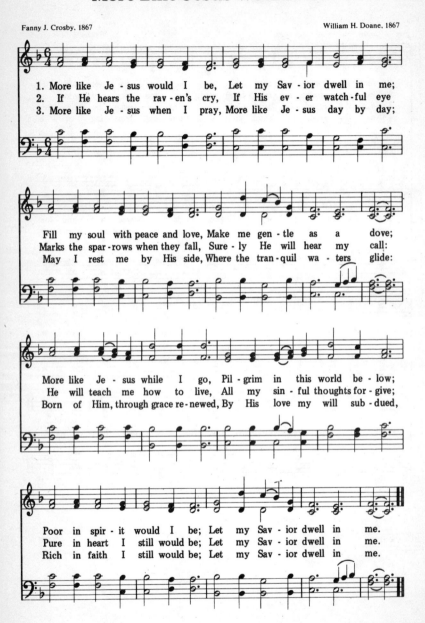

1. More like Je - sus would I be, Let my Sav - ior dwell in me;
2. If He hears the rav - en's cry, If His ev - er watch - ful eye
3. More like Je - sus when I pray, More like Je - sus day by day;

Fill my soul with peace and love, Make me gen - tle as a dove;
Marks the spar - rows when they fall, Sure - ly He will hear my call:
May I rest me by His side, Where the tran - quil wa - ters glide:

More like Je - sus while I go, Pil - grim in this world be - low;
He will teach me how to live, All my sin - ful thoughts for - give;
Born of Him, through grace re - newed, By His love my will sub - dued,

Poor in spir - it would I be; Let my Sav - ior dwell in me.
Pure in heart I still would be; Let my Sav - ior dwell in me.
Rich in faith I still would be; Let my Sav - ior dwell in me.

# Pass Me Not, O Gentle Saviour

Fanny J. Crosby, 1868

William H. Doane, 1870

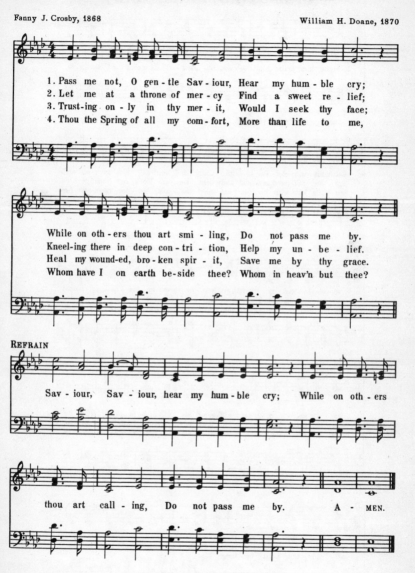

1. Pass me not, O gen-tle Sav-iour, Hear my hum-ble cry;
2. Let me at a throne of mer-cy Find a sweet re-lief;
3. Trust-ing on-ly in thy mer-it, Would I seek thy face;
4. Thou the Spring of all my com-fort, More than life to me,

While on oth-ers thou art smi-ling, Do not pass me by.
Kneel-ing there in deep con-tri-tion, Help my un-be-lief.
Heal my wound-ed, bro-ken spir-it, Save me by thy grace.
Whom have I on earth be-side thee? Whom in heav'n but thee?

**REFRAIN**

Sav-iour, Sav-iour, hear my hum-ble cry; While on oth-ers

thou art call-ing, Do not pass me by. A-MEN.

# Praise Him! Praise Him!

1. Praise him! praise him! Je - sus, our bless - ed Re - deem - er! Sing, O
2. Praise him! praise him! Je - sus, our bless - ed Re - deem - er! For our
3. Praise him! praise him! Je - sus, our bless - ed Re - deem - er! Heav'n - ly

Earth, his won - der - ful love pro - claim! Hail him! hail him! high - est arch-
sins he suf - fered and bled and died; He our Rock, our hope of e-
por - tals loud with ho - san - nas ring! Je - sus, Sav - ior, reign - eth for-

an - gels in glo - ry, Strength and hon - or give to his ho - ly name!
ter - nal sal - va - tion, Hail him! hail him! Je - sus the cru - ci - fied:
ev - er and ev - er; Crown him! crown him! proph - et and priest and King!

Like a shep - herd, Je - sus will guard his chil - dren; In his arms he
Sound his prais - es! Je - sus who bore our sor - rows, Love un - bound - ed,
Christ is com - ing, o - ver the world vic - to - rious, Pow'r and glo - ry

car - ries them all day long:
won - der - ful, deep, and strong: Praise him! praise him! tell of his
un - to the Lord be - long:

ex - cel - lent great - ness! Praise him! praise him! ev - er in joy - ful song!

# Redeemed, How I Love to Proclaim It

Words, Fanny J. Crosby, 1882.

William J. Kirkpatrick, 1882.

# Rescue the Perishing

Fanny J. Crosby, 1869

William H. Doane, 1870

1. Res-cue the per-ish-ing, care for the dy-ing, Snatch them in pit-y from sin and the grave; Weep o'er the err-ing one, lift up the fall-en, Tell them of Je-sus the might-y to save.
2. Though they are slight-ing Him, still He is wait-ing, Wait-ing the pen-i-tent child to re-ceive; Plead with them ear-nest-ly, plead with them gen-tly, He will for-give if they on-ly be-lieve.
3. Down in the hu-man heart, crushed by the tempt-er, Feel-ings lie bur-ied that grace can re-store; Touched by a lov-ing heart, wak-ened by kind-ness, Cords that are bro-ken will vi-brate once more.
4. Res-cue the per-ish-ing, du-ty de-mands it; Strength for thy la-bor the Lord will pro-vide; Back to the nar-row way pa-tient-ly win them; Tell the poor wan-d'rer a Sav-ior has died.

*Refrain*

Res-cue the per-ish-ing, care for the dy-ing; Je-sus is mer-ci-ful, Je-sus will save.

# Saved by Grace

Fanny J. Crosby 1893

Alt. by Seymour Swets, 1934

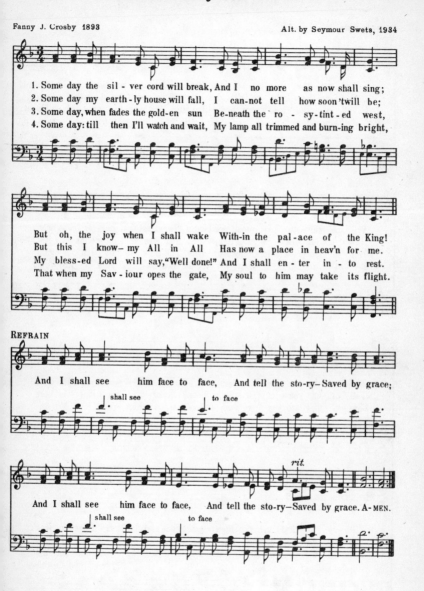

1. Some day the sil - ver cord will break, And I no more as now shall sing;
2. Some day my earth - ly house will fall, I can - not tell how soon 'twill be;
3. Some day, when fades the gold-en sun Be-neath the ro - sy-tint-ed west,
4. Some day: till then I'll watch and wait, My lamp all trimmed and burn-ing bright,

But oh, the joy when I shall wake With-in the pal - ace of the King!
But this I know— my All in All Has now a place in heav'n for me.
My bless-ed Lord will say, "Well done!" And I shall en - ter in - to rest.
That when my Sav - iour opes the gate, My soul to him may take its flight.

**REFRAIN**

And I shall see him face to face, And tell the sto-ry— Saved by grace;

shall see   to face

And I shall see him face to face, And tell the sto-ry— Saved by grace. A-MEN.

shall see   to face

*rit.*

# Tell Me the Story of Jesus

Fanny J. Crosby, 1880

John R. Sweney, 1880

# Though Your Sins Be as Scarlet

Fanny J. Crosby, 1820 - 1915

Alt. by Henry J. Van Andel

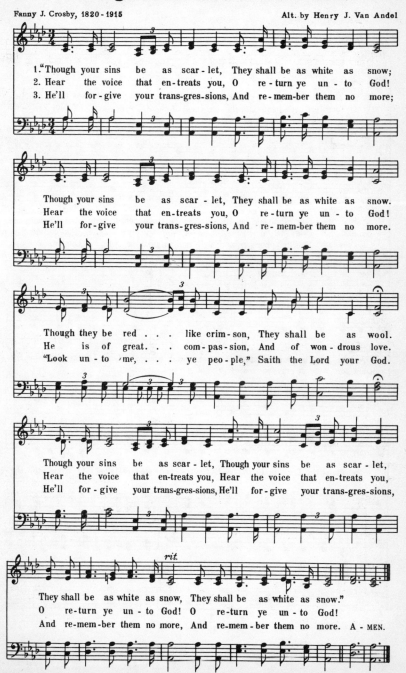

1. "Though your sins be as scar-let, They shall be as white as snow;
2. Hear the voice that en-treats you, O re-turn ye un-to God!
3. He'll for-give your trans-gres-sions, And re-mem-ber them no more;

Though your sins be as scar-let, They shall be as white as snow.
Hear the voice that en-treats you, O re-turn ye un-to God!
He'll for-give your trans-gres-sions, And re-mem-ber them no more.

Though they be red . . . like crim-son, They shall be as wool.
He is of great . . . com-pas-sion, And of won-drous love.
"Look un-to me, . . . ye peo-ple," Saith the Lord your God.

Though your sins be as scar-let, Though your sins be as scar-let,
Hear the voice that en-treats you, Hear the voice that en-treats you,
He'll for-give your trans-gres-sions, He'll for-give your trans-gres-sions,

*rit.*

They shall be as white as snow, They shall be as white as snow."
O re-turn ye un-to God! O re-turn ye un-to God!
And re-mem-ber them no more, And re-mem-ber them no more. A - MEN.

# To God Be the Glory

Fanny J. Crosby, 1875

William H. Doane, 1875

1. To God be the glo - ry, great things He hath done, So loved He the world that He
2. O per - fect re - demp - tion, the pur-chase of blood, To ev - er - y be - liev - er the
3. Great things He hath taught us, great things He hath done, And great our re-joic - ing thro'

gave us His Son, Who yield-ed His life an a - tone-ment for sin, And o-pened the
prom-ise of God; The vil - est of - fend - er who tru - ly be-lieves, That mo-ment from
Je - sus the Son; But pur - er, and high - er, and great - er will be Our won-der, our

*Refrain*

Life-gate that all may go in.
Je - sus a par-don re-ceives. Praise the Lord, praise the Lord, Let the earth hear His
trans-port, when Je - sus we see.

voice! Praise the Lord, praise the Lord, Let the peo - ple re-joice! O come to the

Fa-ther thro' Je - sus the Son, And give Him the glo - ry, great things He hath done.